Men Are Like Mocha Lattes

LISA SUMMERS

MEN ARE LIKE MOCHA LATTES

2007

Men Are Like Mocha Lattes

TABLE OF CONTENTS

ACKNOWLEDGEMENTS

A big "thank you" to Gord Steventon for his amazing work, and to Thelma Barer-Stein for her encouragement. A special "thank you" to Phil Johnson for coaching me through the writing process, and to Kristin Holbrook, Helen Risteen and Lynn Eang.

I would also like to thank my parents, Mary and Terry, for their love, support, and for lending me their Blockbuster card when needed. And finally, a very special "thank you" to my husband Lyle, for his love, patience, support, and for proving there still are a few good men out there.

To My Best Friend
Lyle
With Love

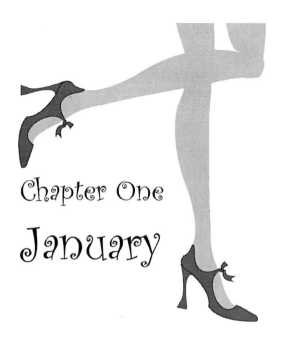

Chapter One

January

An Adventure of a Lifetime

Dear Diary,

I'm stranded at an airport in Fiji and I think I'm going to die of heat stroke. Then again, I might die of dehydration first. There doesn't seem to be anywhere to buy a bottle of water. Amazingly, the best part of this trip so far has been passing through American customs. I credit Bobbi Brown's make-up artist, Bess. I was so happy with the results of the under-eye concealer she recommended, I was apparently glowing. The customs officers all smiled at me and wished me a good vacation as they waved me through. It was amazing. I suddenly had all of this self-assurance radiating from within, for the cost of a concealer and a $10 tip at the make-up counter. Who says you can't buy confidence in a bottle?

I had an uneventful flight from Toronto to Los Angeles, then passed through customs to board my flight to Nadi, which is when the demise of my adventure of a lifetime began. Our flight was delayed and I hadn't realized that my trip from Toronto to L.A. had been five and a half, not two and a half hours long, with a three-hour time difference. I was confused beyond reason about what time it had been, was, and would be if we (ever) landed in Fiji.

I was sweating and overheated and desperately wishing I had bought a "Los Angeles" T-shirt when I had the chance to at the gift shop. Instead, I bought a copy of Martin Seligman's book, Authentic Happiness, *which only added weight to my luggage and made me sweat even more.*

And so I suffered in my newly bought, over-priced Guess? sweater. And just when I thought things couldn't get worse, because I was so tired and hungry, and because my back felt like it was going to snap under the weight of my laptop carry case and all the books, magazines and food I was carrying, my newly purchased pink Guess? bag snapped instead.

It was highly symbolic: a break from American fashion trends and the coming of spring, when advice from E. Jean Carroll of Elle Magazine *and her new book would help me find* Mr. Right, Right Now!*...all gone with a sudden snap.*

No longer was I a young, under-employed lawyer, somehow always able to afford a new purse or sun vacation, but a student. A broke student. With a broken strap. For the rest of the journey, other passengers kept saying, "Excuse me, did you know your strap is broken?"

I wanted to say, YES! YES! It's broke! Just like me! I realize. I've just made a terrible mistake!

Instead, I smiled graciously and said nothing.

It was a somewhat impulsive decision to leave Toronto to study at a teacher's college in New Zealand. Like it or not, I turn thirty this year, and I'm the last of my circle of friends from high school to be single. I hate being single. I'm determined to get married before I enter a new decade, when, according to Elle Magazine, *I have to start wearing "age-appropriate" clothing. Then, after throwing away all of my mini-skirts so that I don't embarrass myself or others around me, I would be wise to start fertility contingency-planning, i.e., making appointments to have my ovaries frozen, putting my name on international adoption lists, and weighing the pros and cons of raising a child on my own. Of course, as one cunning* Elle *writer suggested, I could always just sleep with a man without using any contraception to impregnate myself and force him into eighteen years of child support payments. A tempting idea, but I'd better not.*

***

After a long ten-hour flight, we arrived to the stunning beauty of the Fiji Islands. As we landed, everyone stood to look out the windows to get a better view of the sparkling turquoise water and white sandy beaches below.

We were delayed in Nadi for several more hours. I thought I was going to die in the heat, sweating in my Guess? sweater and listening to the arrogant ravings of someone who can only be described as Not Good Looking At All (which is a horrible thing to say, but he was a horrible person).

Not Good Looking At All was yelling at the Air Pacific staff to figure out why the hell we (in transit passengers) weren't being taken care of to catch our connecting flight to Wellington.

Because he had a wedding to go to.

His own.

And he hadn't been able to smoke the entire flight over and there was no smoking in the airport—could they comprehend the need for a cigarette?

Now?

Jesus.

He was going to be late for his own *?#$*! wedding.

I could swear to God he was another lawyer. I would bet my entire life's savings, but since I have none, I would bet my parents'.

All the while that no one was serving us and my fellow dehydrated, hungry and tired passengers were becoming increasingly upset, three men in tropical shirts and long black skirts and sandals were singing loudly in the center of the airport and playing musical instruments. Not Good Looking At All was Not Amused.

The men kept pointing at me and saying *Bula*. I had no idea whether it was a compliment or an insult. I decided to take it as a compliment.

There was a hurricane.

We couldn't land in Wellington.

Probable Lawyer/Not Good Looking At All was so agitated, I was sure he was bursting blood vessels in his brain. I wondered what his fiancée was like. I decided I was "authentically happy" being single.

My Big Fat Greek Welcome

Drew's mother is Greek. He warned me so many times. *She's Greek,* he kept saying in the car, while nervously chewing the end of a ragged fingernail. Drew is my new "flat mate" who came to pick me up when I finally arrived in Wellington after an overnight stay at Christchurch airport. I had been forced to wait until two o'clock in the afternoon to catch my connecting flight. Probable Lawyer had almost tackled another passenger to the ground when he tried to move to the head of the line to board an earlier flight this morning. I decided it probably wasn't worth it to argue the merits of letting ladies go first.

"I just want you to be prepared before you meet her."

Drew was making such a strong case for how unbearably loud and controlling his mother is, that I started to feel nervous. Cold droplets of sweat trickled down my back as the blazing Kiwi sun beat down on the roof of Drew's white Nissan hatchback.

We had spent the past fifteen minutes chatting about Drew's family, which currently consists of his son, three-year-old Miles, his estranged wife Janine, his mother Helena, his grandmother Yolanda, and his brother, Owen.

I turned to look at him from where I sat in my passenger seat. His striking green eyes were now hidden behind a pair of mirrored aviator sunglasses. Glints of auburn flecked his dark ash brown hair, shaved close to the nape of his neck. Jaw tightly clenched, he kept both hands on the steering wheel, and I could just make out a thin tan line on his wedding ring finger.

It was a strange experience to be driving on the left-hand side of the road, which was lined with tall palm trees, branches swaying lazily in the warm wind. Flowering evergreen shrubs with large, shiny leaves were punctuated by bright fuchsia blossoms that decorated the foliage like tropical ornaments on a Christmas tree.

Drew warned me, for what seemed like the hundredth time, that life with his mother is always dramatic. I assured him that I had plenty of experience with Greek mothers.

Not this Greek mother. As soon as we walked through the door, we were greeted by complete pandemonium. Assorted socks and underwear were strewn across the furniture in the living room, where an ancient-looking vacuum cleaner stood, motor running, by the window. A well-fed calico kitten was energetically scratching the faded curtains that looked to be moments away from landing in a heap on the floor.

Drew's little boy, Miles, was in a very excited state and seemed to have consumed vast quantities of sugar, judging by the half-empty boxes of chocolate-covered digestives and Cadbury Pinky Treats on the kitchen table.

"Daddy! Daddy!" he shrieked when he saw us, running to throw himself into Drew's arms.

Drew's mother, a fifty-ish meat-and-potatoes-looking woman with Titian red hair, wearing a white pleated apron over her dress, walked over to turn off the vacuum cleaner and shoo the kitten from the curtains. She began talking a mile a minute to Drew, gesturing wildly, huge blue eyes threatening to fall out of their sockets.

I felt the sudden urge to grab my suitcases and run. (Of course, my suitcases are so heavy this would have defied the laws of gravity.) Drew had already had a huge "row" with Helena that morning and was apparently on the verge of some sort of nervous breakdown. He left me at her mercy in the living room while leading away a sticky-fingered Miles. Helena motioned for me to sit on a black faux-leather couch while she settled herself on the matching love seat in front of the window.

Before I could think of anything to say, she suddenly sprang back up from her seat, screaming, "DREW! DREW! DREW!" with a look of sheer terror on her face. I couldn't imagine what catastrophe had just struck but I prepared for the Rapture (which would be a catastrophe because I've been flirting with atheism for the past three months).

It was the washing machine. Soapy water was rapidly flooding the tiny kitchen floor and rushing towards us at a frightening speed. I looked over at my monogrammed designer luggage by the door, and then back at the approaching tidal wave of suds.

I knew I shouldn't have brought my good luggage.

Damn.

"DREW!" I yelled.

Drew ran into the kitchen to see what was happening, while Helena continued to scream. A bare-bottomed Miles joined us, jumping up and down, clapping his hands, and shrieking in between bursts of giggles. I closed my eyes and said a silent prayer, promising God that I would start reading the Bible again every week, or at least once a month, if He would just spare my designer luggage.

I opened my eyes to see Drew wading through the kitchen into the laundry room. He reached into the sink next to the washing machine and pulled out a thick piece of cardboard, which Helena had placed over the top of the drain for reasons that apparently made sense at the time. After he turned off the washing machine, the flooding gradually subsided. I breathed a sigh of relief that my luggage was still dry.

Assessing the scene before me, I decided it would be a good idea to leave the house before anything else went wrong. Helena was still in an agitated state as she grabbed an armful of towels to mop up the floor. The more excited, loud and intense she became, the more I felt my own nervous breakdown could be just around the corner. (And the more I began to doubt a mere genetic pre-disposition towards "excitability" inherited by her New Zealand-born, "Greek" father, which had been Drew's less-than convincing explanation for her demeanour).

In Toronto, identifying as Greek means:

(a) You just arrived to Canada from Greece with or without your parents

(b) You arrived from Greece when you were six with your parents, or

(c) One parent is actually from Greece.

Just as I was about to open the front door, Miles caught me by the sleeve.

"Lindsay! Can you...play with me?"

I looked down at the cocoa-haired imp in front of me, pink-cheeked and eyes sparkling. Taking advantage of my hesitation, Miles dragged me to the bathroom where he announced that he wanted to have a bath. I could hear Helena and Drew arguing upstairs and wondered whether it was an ominous foreshadowing. If every weekend was like this, I didn't see myself being able to study. I hadn't felt entirely confident about moving in with Drew, especially after finding out that he was embroiled in a messy separation.

At that moment the telephone rang, and Miles ran from the bathroom, quickly returning with a cordless receiver in his hand, which he offered to me.

The voices upstairs were growing louder and I heard Helena say, "...completely irresponsible! I won't keep bailing you out like this! Do you understand? I've driven six hours from Hamilton..."

"I didn't ask you to drive six hours from Hamilton! I could have done without you flooding my kitchen, thank you very much!"

"Your kitchen? *Your* kitchen? Who paid for this house? Who's providing for your son and paying your lawyer's fees and..."

"Hello?" I grabbed the ringing phone from Miles' hand.

"Who is this?" The female voice on the other end of the line sounded suspicious.

"It's Lindsay. Who's this?"

"It's Janine. I'm Miles' mother. Who are you?"

"I'm the Canadian student staying at the house."

"You're *what?* Put my husband on the phone!"

I could hear Helena and Drew still arguing upstairs. I watched as Miles expertly fit the rubber stopper over the drain in the bathtub, and turned both faucets on.

"I'm sorry, Drew's busy..."

"Oh he is, is he? Busy doing what?" she snapped.

"He's with—his mum," I stammered, feeling myself begin to lose what little composure I had started with.

"With his Mum?" Janine's voice rose to a brittle edge. "You mean Helena's up for the weekend?"

"Umm..."

"The answer is *yes* or *no.*"

"Yes."

"Well, Libby..."

"Lindsay."

"We'll see about all of this. No one told me anything about a Canadian student. You tell Drew and Helena that I'll be ringing my solicitor first thing Monday morning."

"I really don't think..."

"And tell them that all of you are going to pay for the consequences of my decision."

Click.

The line went dead.

Consequences of *what* decision?

Drew suddenly appeared at the door, surprising me. We both looked at Miles who was happily splashing in the bathtub. Drew smiled and said, "He likes taking baths. Are you OK with him?"

What I wanted to say was, *No! I have classes to prepare for on Monday, and it's not my responsibility to look after your son while you fight with your mother!*

What I ended up saying was, "Sure. By the way, Janine phoned."

Drew's smile quickly vanished and furrows of worry lines creased his forehead.

"What did she say?"

"Well…I think she was surprised I'm here. She said to tell you she'll be calling her lawyer, Monday."

"DREW! I'm going to pick up supper. Is Lindsay eating with us?" Helena's voice boomed from upstairs.

"I really…"

Drew's eyes pleaded with me to say, *yes*.

Oh, God. What have I got myself into?

"Sounds great," I lied.

"Ok Mum! Get some extra fish and chips!"

Drew looked visibly relieved and stepped closer to put his hand on my shoulder. I could smell the warm, spicy scent of his cologne and noticed the top buttons of his polo shirt were undone. A slow, sexy smile stretched across his face, and my heart fluttered for a second in my chest.

"Don't worry about Janine. She's just being a jealous ex-wife," he said conspiratorially.

"Gum?" I quickly reached into my pocket and pulled out a wrinkled packet of Dentyne.

"Can I have some gum, Daddy? Can I have some gum?"

Miles was eagerly climbing out of the tub, as fast as his chubby legs would carry him.

"DREW! Have you moved your car? I haven't got all day!" Helena was heavily making her way down the stairs.

Riiiiing!

It was the phone again.

"Do you mind getting that Lindsay? You're a peach." Drew winked and quickly ducked out of the bathroom, leaving me to answer the phone and figure out what to do with the soaking wet toddler in front of me.

And what to do to prevent this trip from turning into a complete and utter catastrophe.

***

11:00 pm

Dear Diary,

I just realized that I forgot to return my *Sex and the City* DVDs to the video store before I left home. I found the "to do" list that I made before leaving Toronto in my purse this evening.

Things to Do For Trip to New Zealand:
1. Return *Sex and the City* DVDs to Blockbuster Video
2. Go to Bobbie Brown book signing and ask advice about getting a new under-eye concealer—do NOT cave and buy anything else
3. Phone the Law Society to inform them I'll be out of the country
4. Send group email letting friends know I'm going to New Zealand for the year
5. Buy lots of green tea to take to New Zealand in case they don't have it there
6. Cancel gym membership before next payment is due!!!
7. Stock up on Dentyne chewing gum to take to New Zealand in case they don't have it there
8. Ask Nathan what the word "Maori" means
9. Look for map of New Zealand on the Internet and try to find Wellington
10. Buy new underwear so I don't embarrass myself with my old holey underwear if I have to share laundry facilities
11. Don't forget about the *Sex and the City* DVDs!!

Damn. Now Blockbuster will realize that I'm not "Terry" Breyer when they call to find out what happened to the late rentals. And my father (Terry) will realize that:

a) I "borrowed" his Blockbuster card
b) He is responsible for my late fees, and
c) There is nothing he can do about it because I am in New Zealand.

Well, the last statement is not strictly true. He could cut off his financial support for this year. But he wouldn't. Would he?

After a tension-filled supper this evening, that included Miles insisting on chocolate syrup in his milk while Helena alternately cursed Janine for ruining his health, and scolded Drew for watching rugby at the table, I excused myself to my bedroom to rest. Helena warned me not to go to sleep too early or I would never get over my jet lag.

I'm beginning to think that wrapping up my life in two months to board a plane for New Zealand was perhaps not the wisest decision, especially given the living accommodation that I find myself in. Jay, the international recruiter who convinced me to embark on this "adventure of a lifetime" promised me that teacher's college would be a "piece of cake". I hope he's right.

Affirmations
This is the best year of my life
I am a brave, confident, capable woman
Each and every moment of my life,
Brings the possibility of meeting Mr. Right

Mind Over Marriage
Well, today I'm ready to throw my copy of this month's "O" magazine out the window. I was settling into bed tonight after a good half hour of stretching and affirmations,
I am in total synchronicity with all of life's possibilities
I wait in serene stillness, knowing my husband is on the way...
when I decided to have a quick glance at an article on "Looking for Happiness in All the Right Places". It's a synopsis of Martin Seligman's theory about genetic set points of subjective well-being (SWB). His conclusion: The single consistent factor in many studies of SWB is the deep embrace of love.

There's more.

"Friends are good, but family's better," says a University of Southern California professor of economics. A survey found that forty-one per cent of Americans who were married described themselves as "very happy" while only twenty-two per cent of those never married, divorced, separated or widowed could say the same thing.

Uh—did I mention that the entire point of this issue of "O" is to help people achieve happiness, and not slip into a quicksand of misery and suicide after the trauma of Valentine's Day?

Dr. Seligman suggests that an "interesting question" has been raised: Whether married people are happier because they're married or whether they were happier in the first place? Here's an interesting thought: Maybe unmarried people are so unhappy because there's so much Pressure to get married in the first place.

I remember going to an interview shortly after being called to the Bar (of Ontario, not for another drink on my way to joining the masses of alcoholic lawyers in the province). When I arrived at the office, I was greeted by a former classmate from law school. Before I continue, I should be honest and confess that I could never stand this woman. She always thought she was God's gift to men. Apparently that attitude works, because there she was, waving her left hand conspicuously, talking a mile a minute about her fairy tale honeymoon in Hawaii and pausing for only a moment to ask if I was "with" anyone.

No, not at the moment, I mumbled.

"Well!" she said, eyes gleaming triumphantly, licking her lips like a cat in front of the cream bowl.

"That's too bad. Married life is *wonderful*. I *highly* recommend it."

I said nothing. How could I? An unmarried woman, after all. Sour grapes, etc. Even Julia Roberts had an unconvincing Mona Lisa smile at the end of her movie. The student who turned down law school at Yale to be a housewife seemed like the most authentically happy character.

I should write my own article, pointing out the myriad of sociological studies of divorce rates, and tales of marital misery. I should also write to Martin Seligman and point out the numerous cases of suicidal, anguished mothers who were brilliant yet felt compelled to drown themselves in the river or put their heads in the oven. (An interesting question: were they disturbed before or after the wedding?) But now, I just sound like the bitter old spinster my first boyfriend told me I would become, when I wouldn't sleep with him.

Advanced Affirmations
I believe in miracles, and I now welcome their manifesting
Each and every moment of my life,
Brings the possibility of meeting Mr. Right

In Hot Water With Helena
My laundry is ruined. My once-white socks and bras are now various shades of fuchsia. The worst part is that my Christian Dior sweater is no longer ivory, but shocking pink. It was my favorite piece of clothing; my ex-boyfriend Ben gave it to me as a birthday present after a trip to Paris. I've always been vigilant about making sure that it's properly washed and cared for.

I almost had a heart attack when Helena came to my room with the laundry basket. She had insisted on washing my clothes for me, even though I had insisted just as vocally that I prefer to do my laundry myself. She told me it was easier to wash my clothes with everyone else's and since hot water is more expensive here than at home, I didn't argue.

"Lindsay, I wasn't sure what to do with these, were you wanting to keep them?"

Helena was holding up three pairs of sorry-looking underwear that looked like a tie-dye experiment gone awry. They had large, gaping holes in the crotch and the elastics had gone on them. *Damn*. It had completely slipped my mind to buy myself some new underclothes before leaving Toronto.

I've noticed that Helena is very particular about certain things. For instance, she insists on redoing my coffee when I make it. She keeps telling me that I have to put my cream in first, or the coffee won't have a proper froth at the top. I don't see what difference it makes because it tastes the same to me. But apparently, this is how a "flat white" is properly made (a "flat white" is the Kiwi expression for a coffee with milk and sugar).

Six days after landing in Wellington, my body clock still hasn't adjusted. I find myself wanting to fall asleep during the day, and then feeling wide awake at night. I also find myself feeling hungry at about 10 pm, so I've been sneaking into the fridge late at night, trying to find whatever I can to stop my stomach from rumbling. The past two nights that I've gone into the kitchen, Helena has suddenly appeared to ask what's wrong, and why I'm eating more cookies that are only going to make me fat. She thinks I should be eating more at dinner. I wish the woman would go back to Hamilton, but she wants to be here when Drew's other flat mate arrives.

I've realized that since Helena sleeps with the bedroom door open, I'm going to have to think of another way to deal with this situation. I've made a mental note to myself to buy some "crisps" at school tomorrow so I can hide them under my bed.

9:12 pm

I have to present a teaching lesson in Social Studies class tomorrow and I can't sleep. I hate talking in class, which is not like me at all. I've been feeling self-conscious about my "American accent."

9:32 pm

I'm hungry. I keep thinking about the cookies in the kitchen.

9:45 pm

I have to stop thinking about those cookies. Think about something else, Lindsay. Hmmm...sex. Well that's great—I can't have any of that either.

9:50 pm

Cookies, cookies, cookies.

9:55 pm

It's quiet. I think Helena's gone to sleep. Maybe if I tiptoe, she won't wake up.

10:03 pm

She woke up. I was apprehended in the kitchen with my hands literally in the cookie jar. Wearing a pink floral nightgown with puffy short sleeves, Helena loudly asked me what was wrong. I told her nothing was wrong. I was just getting a snack because I was hungry. She looked at the plate of cookies in my hand.

"They'll make you fat!"

I wasn't sure what to say and stood there nervously, blinking in the glare of the hallway light that she had switched on. Helena told me that I should eat more during dinner. I promised her I would have a larger helping next time, and apologized for waking her up. She looked at me suspiciously as I shivered, teeth chattering, in my thin cotton pyjamas. The temperature is freezing at night, but I thought it would be rude to keep complaining. Helena has insisted on making my bed herself and she bought an expensive down lining to put on top of the mattress.

"But you can't be cold!" She'd protest every morning after I'd ask if I could buy myself an electric blanket.

"Look at you shaking! It's all the espresso and sugar!"

"I'm actually just feeling a bit co..."

"Make sure you're on time and don't keep Drew waiting in the morning! You've got to put your A into G, Lindsay."

"Right. What does that mean?"

"Arse into gear."

"Right."

I heard Drew snicker, and I silently cursed him as I beat a hasty retreat back to my bedroom. Damn him.

13

11:00 pm

I'm hungry again. This is torture. I should have just taken more cookies since I got caught anyway.

11:10 pm

Sex.

Sex, sex, sex.

11:29 pm

I have six and a half hours until I have to be up to start getting ready for school. Even if I fall asleep right now, I'll still be short by one and a half hours. They say that people who get less than eight hours of sleep a night are more prone to be depressed, have accidents, and gain weight.

11:45 pm

I hope my lecturer, Marion, doesn't say anything to embarrass me tomorrow. On Monday, she referred to me as "Lindsay, with the lovely curly hair". Jordy, one of the guys in my class, looked at me and snickered.

1:00 am

I've singed my hair. I was in the bathroom and found a curling iron that must have belonged to Janine. I decided to try to smooth my hair. I guess I'm not used to the "professional" strength heat—well, I haven't really used a curling iron since high school. Anyway, now the ends of my hair are burned.

1:10 am

I hate New Zealand.

Affirmations

I wait in serene stillness, knowing my husband is on the way

Everyday, in every way,

My stay in New Zealand gets better and better

"O" No, What Have I Done?

The enormity of my decision to leave home for a year hit at noon today, when I suddenly developed a migraine and thought I was going to faint. At that very moment, George, my International Languages instructor, suddenly whipped out a series of yellow cards and began an unexpected lesson in an Indonesian dialect without using a word of English. I wanted to shrivel up and die like one of the oranges I zealously buy to increase my store of antioxidants, and then forget about in the fridge for weeks until someone else finds them.

It was horrible. It was beyond horrible. I had a vivid image of the latest issue of "O" magazine that is full of Dr. Martin Seligman's happiness theories. The cover is bright yellow and Oprah is wearing a sweat suit the color of a very ripe orange.

It was an interesting "aha" moment. One of those moments when I'd like to see Oprah transported to Wellington, minus her millions/billions of dollars. How would she cope, suddenly thrust into a classroom with a hard-nosed New Zealander pouncing on her to answer his questions in Indonesian? This, without the cameras rolling, without photos or other evidence of her unprecedented birthday party of the century, or her audience full of adoring fans. Would she be gracious, sitting in the humidity with a pounding head covered in uncontrollably frizzy hair? Would she really be able to smile her all-knowing, I-have-an-award-for-humanitarianism smile?

Humph! I don't think so.

Emergency Affirmations
I am comfortably and easily adapting to life in New Zealand
I am not jealous of Oprah Winfrey
I am a brave, confident, capable woman

A Born-Again Virgin
Dear Nathan,
Hi! How's it goin'? I'm sorry to hear things didn't work out with Andrea. Long-distance relationships can be hard, especially when you meet over the Internet. I can understand why you're no longer a fan of born-again Christians, but I don't actually think her religion had anything to do with the break up. No offence, but if my ex-fiancé suddenly showed up and announced I could have a new BMW along with my diamond ring, I'd be pretty tempted as well. Five years is a lot of history to compete with (not to mention the man's bank account).

Cheer up! At least you don't have to pretend to read the Bible anymore.

Just reading over your email…Do I think she dumped you because you were too honest? Well, maybe the next time a religious girl asks about your sexual history, you can just say you're a "born again virgin". That's what I do.

Seriously Nathan, don't be so hard on yourself. The odds weren't on your side, Big Brother.

Speaking of odd, our new flat mate moved in yesterday. His name is Bryce and he's South African. Helena kept saying she hoped he wouldn't be too much of a "boar". If she meant aggressive, she's right! He was totally hitting on me at dinner tonight. He kept asking if I'd tried a Speights yet (Kiwi beer), and then not so casually started talking about how he's looking for a girlfriend "purely for the sake of marriage and children," while waggling his eyebrows at me. You should see him, Nathan! He looks exactly like my first crush—six feet tall, super skinny, with curlier hair than mine. I think he's probably about thirty-five.

Anyway, tonight was hilarious. Bryce has a really sarcastic sense of humor and I can tell he's already getting under Drew's skin. We were sitting in the living room watching rugby, and Miles kept asking for a cookie, but Drew told him he had to wait until after dinner. As soon as Drew went to the washroom, Bryce grabbed some chocolate cookies from the jar, and gave them to Miles. When Drew came back he looked totally stunned to see Miles grinning at him with chocolate all over his face and his new red corduroy overalls. Bryce looked at Drew and said, "Poor lad was hungry. Don't mind if he has a few biscuits, eh mate? Unless—you want him to starve." And then he looked at me, with a wicked grin on his face. Drew was livid.

Anyway, Bryce drove me to school this morning. He's got this old, beat- up red Jeep with no doors, but he put his sunglasses on, cranked up the radio and drove it like he thought it was a Maserati. On the way in, he hit a speed bump hard, and I spilled coffee all over my white cashmere skirt. Bryce looked and me and said, "She's alright, luv. Daddy will buy you a new one." Then, he flashed me the same wicked grin. I wanted to strangle him! That skirt cost me $300! I don't know why, but he's convinced our family has tons of money. (I know what you're going to say—it's the designer luggage.)

So anyway, this afternoon Drew decided that all three of us should go shopping for bedroom furniture. We went to a consignment shop that was barely lit inside. It smelled like a combination of mothballs and curry. Nearly all of the mattresses were stained, and I could tell Bryce knew I didn't want to buy anything.

A Pakistani salesman came up to us, and the first thing Bryce said was, "Hi, mate. We're looking for a bed, for her. She's a bit fussy about… everything really. She's Canadian."

Before I could think of a response, the salesman turned to me and exclaimed,

"An American! This is very exciting! I have a son who just turned your age, Miss. He will make you a wonderful husband if I can just..."

"That's ok, that's ok!" I interrupted. "I'm actually not feeling very well. We should get going. Thank you for your help."

"Thank you very often."

In other news, Janine left another lovely message on the answering machine today (Don't tell Mom!) It went something like, "Hello Libby, how are we today? Enjoying New Zealand? Miles talks about you, you know. He tells me everything. So we fancy my husband, do we? I will drive you straight back to Canada, you American tart! I will chop all of your hair off! I will—Mum! Give me back the phone!"

Click.

I don't know whether I should be worried. Helena said something strange before she went to back to Hamilton. She and Drew had a huge fight over whether Miles is allowed to have chocolate syrup in his milk. Before she left, she told Drew not to expect any paid holidays this year. Drew snapped, "I'd rather spend Christmas alone, thank you very much," which didn't seem wise to me since they have vacation property in Fiji. (Personally, I would have just tossed out the chocolate syrup instead of missing out on a sun vacation. But that's just me.) Anyway, before Helena left, she added, "I hope you'll be alright Lindsay. You're a very pretty girl and Janine can get jealous."

(!)

It's weird. I don't understand how such a rich family can have so many problems. Helena comes from "Greek" wealth and apparently all of Drew's cousins have made millions running their own businesses in Wellington. But Drew doesn't seem to have any money of his own, which might explain the lack of funds to heat the house.

Well Big Brother, I better get back to my International Languages assignment. George, my instructor, doesn't seem to like me, for some reason. He keeps handing back my work and telling me I don't understand the instructions, but I'm pretty sure I do. I've noticed a lot of people here don't seem to like "Americans". I keep pointing out that Canada is a separate country and we're Canadian, not American. But Drew says it's all the same thing.

On that note, I hope that love and happiness are just around the corner for both of us, my fellow Canadian!

Love,

Lindsay

P.S. Thanks for the information about the Maori. I had no idea there was an indigenous tribe in New Zealand before I came here. I really have to get up to speed on things. I was joining another group of students at lunch today, and everyone looked shocked when I sat on top of the picnic table. George was walking by at that moment and yelled, "Get down from that picnic table!" I was totally confused, and Sydney, one of the girls in my class, pulled me aside and explained that it's offensive in Maori culture to have body parts below the waist, near food—or something like that. Of course, the picnic table area is right in front of the Maori Cultural Centre on campus, so I couldn't have chosen a better location to be an offensive "American".

I think I'm going through a steep learning curve right now. To be honest Nathan, New Zealand isn't really what I expected. I hope I can make it through the year.

Dear Mom & Dad,

Hi! Hope everyone's well! Glad to hear Dad enjoyed his retirement party. New Zealand is really beautiful and classes are great!

Having a wonderful time.

Love,

Lindsay

The Surreal Life

Dear Diary,

I finally feel defeated. I've been arriving late for class every day, and I can't even concentrate enough to read, let alone hand in assignments. My hair looks terrifying. It's bigger and frizzier than I've ever seen it before. Maybe it wouldn't be such a bad thing if Janine chopped it off, after all. Last night, I "fell" into the toilet again, and Drew and Bryce have been drinking all of my green tea. Every morning when I wake up, my eyes are bloodshot and my head is pounding from allergies. It turns out that New Zealand is known for having strong pollen and many foreigners with no previous allergies develop them after moving here.

George, my International Languages instructor, filed a complaint about me to the school administration over the picnic table incident. This resulted in my being "advised" to see one of the counselors in student health services to "smooth" my transition to student life in New Zealand. I was fifteen minutes late getting to my appointment because Bryce overslept this morning. As soon as we pulled into the parking lot, I jumped out of the jeep and sprinted to the other side of the campus, tripping over a loose shoelace on my way. By the time I arrived at student health services, my face was the color of a raspberry, I had sweat stains under my arms, and a fresh hole in my jeans which were torn during the fall.

When I finally arrived at her office, Beatrice, the guidance counselor, looked at me disapprovingly over the tops of her bifocals. Her silver-white hair was almost as frizzy as mine, and fell in wiry curls to her shoulders. She wore enormous gold hoop earrings that tugged painfully on her earlobes, strings of orange and yellow beads around her neck, bangles of assorted primary colors on her arms, a large orange caftan, and Birkenstocks. She motioned for me to sit, and when she settled herself into her wicker armchair and arranged her feet on the resting block in front of her, I had a clear view of her unshaven legs.

"Lindsay," she said evenly.

"Beatrice."

She glanced at the torn hole in my jeans and we both looked at the angry red bubbles of blood forming on my knee.

"Oh my, have you hurt yourself?" she asked, wrinkling her nose.

She got up heavily to retrieve some tissue from her desk and came back to hand it to me, gingerly.

"I tripped on my way here," I explained, dabbing at my knee with the tissue.

"That's unusual. Are you always this clumsy, or was there something in particular that upset you this morning?" She peered at me over her bifocals, pale blue eyes gazing intently into mine as though searching for a clue to the dark recesses of my soul.

"Not really. I mean, I'm not usually this clumsy. Well, I guess I— uh. I don't know."

"I see." She sat back in her armchair and wrote something down on a large spiral notepad, then leaned forward again.

"So Lindsay, how can I help you today?"

I looked up at her, and my attention was drawn to a large mole just above her jaw line. It had two dark hairs growing out of it, and I wondered why she didn't trim them. Then again, she doesn't shave her legs, so I guess she's being consistent.

"Well, um...Beatrice."

"Yes?"

She was tapping her pen against the notepad and I could see she had written "Lindsay Breyer" on the top of the page, in big block letters.

"It's just that...Actually, it was administration that told me I should come to see you. What happened was, George..."

"Are you American?" she asked, as though suddenly noticing my accent for the first time.

"No, Canadian."

"It's all the same thing," she said matter-of-factly.

"No one informed me there were American students on campus. How many of you are there?"

"About fifteen altogether, I think."

"Fif-teen!" she exclaimed, drawing out the "teen".

"Fifteen foreign students in a New Zealand education program!" She looked personally insulted and I wasn't sure what to say.

"Foreign students in education! That's preposterous!"

When she said "preposterous" a spray of nicotine-laced saliva showered through the air, and I started to offer her a stick of Dentyne, then thought better of it.

"Twelve months is not enough time for an American to adapt to this country. New Zealand is a very unique country."

She paused expectantly, and I nodded my head in silent, if insincere, agreement.

"We are unique. One year is not long enough for you to adapt to life here and teach our students. Especially not law. I'm going to have you removed from social studies immediately. What is your second teaching subject?"

"French."

"That's acceptable, I suppose."

"What will I take instead of social studies then?"

"Hmm…I see from your student profile that you studied drama in high school. I think our acting coach Dale needs more students. I'll transfer you to a performing arts module for second semester…if you're still with us then."

She closed her notebook and stood up.

"That will be all, Lindsay."

"Should I book another appointment?"

"No, not unless it's completely necessary. Although you really don't seem to be adapting very smoothly to Kiwi life. If you find you can't make the adjustment, I suggest you seriously consider going back home."

"OK."

"Good day, then."

"Good day."

***

And that was my first and last counseling session, which does not bode well for the following reasons:

a) Apparently, I'm not adapting as "smoothly" as I should be to student life in New Zealand
b) Apparently, foreign students, and especially "Americans" are not particularly welcome in this education program, and
c) Apparently, I will have to get used to being called an "American" for the rest of the year.

The thought also occurs to me that Beatrice isn't likely to be supportive if George keeps filing complaints. I went to visit him after leaving her office, to see whether I could "smooth" things over, and found him outside the International Languages Building. He was dressed in a dull brown tweed jacket with mustard-colored patches on the elbow, looking lost in thought as he smoked his pipe.

George seems very nationalistic, maybe even fanatical, which does not bode well for my stay because I keep referring to New Zealanders as Australians. It's totally innocent and probably just a symptom of jet lag. Or it might be because:

a) Nathan kept joking about me going to the "Land Down Under," or because,

b)   On New Year's Eve, I was inspired to create a lofty "to do" list that included visiting Australia, or

c)   It could be due to the sheer confusion over Mel Gibson's true country of origin.

Anyway, apparently I seem to think I'm in Australia. I am not. I am in New Zealand.

I emphatically agreed with George yesterday, that New Zealand and Australia are indeed two separate countries after making the most egregious gaffe possible in his classroom: I corrected myself after referring to a classmate from New Zealand as an Australian.

George hates Australians. He also hates Asians (who form a significant part of the population here—who knew?), South Africans, the Maori, and most of all, he hates President George Bush. He seems to preface every statement with the words, "You Americans..." before launching into a diatribe about the latest way the United States has ruined the world.

Today was no exception. When he saw me, he immediately launched into a rant about George Bush's latest political follies, snapping green eyes bright with anger, gold-rimmed spectacles slipping down his nose as his head shook with emphasis. He paused to ask whether I'd been to my guidance counseling appointment, because it was apparent to him that I required some serious assistance in adapting to student life in New Zealand. I told him that I'd just come from seeing Beatrice, and that seemed to subdue him. Then I made the mistake of trying to appeal to his sense of nationalism. I told him I was enjoying my stay in New Zealand, and that Kiwis and Canadians actually have a lot in common because we both live in the shadow of a larger neighbor.

George turned an even brighter red than his balding hair, and sputtered, "We have bugger-all in common! Americans, Canadians, it's all the same thing! And where is your last assignment? I told you to have it redone and on my desk by nine o'clock this morning!"

Damn.

I was so busy baby-sitting Miles the night before, and getting ready for my counseling session, I'd completely forgotten about redoing the assignment. Not that I thought it needed to be redone. I've tried telling George that I like to be creative with my lesson plans, but he tells me to "Just do what you're told".

Today's Affirmations
I am a strong, confident and capable woman
This is the best year of my life
Every day, in every way,
My life in New Zealand gets better and better

***

Dear Diary,

I hate New Zealand. I hate the sarcasm, I hate the food, and I hate the weather. One minute it's sunny, the next minute there's a torrential downpour. Kiwis are fond of saying that in Auckland, you can have four seasons in one day. I would be happy if they could just get some central heating.

Last night we had a flatmate meeting and Drew tried to establish some house rules. But I don't think Bryce was impressed when he quickly figured out that I had already complained to Drew about the wet laundry in the washer, the toilet seat being left up, and the TV blasting late at night in the living room, which is on the other side of my bedroom wall.

Drew has asked me to draw up a list of household chores that we're supposed to take turns sharing, but I have a feeling I know who will end up doing everything, and it won't be our South African friend who monopolizes the TV and leaves the kitchen counter covered in crumbs. I am amazed at how quickly the kitchen gets invaded by ants when food is left out. We can't even leave unwashed dishes in the sink.

I feel like I'm living in the Third World.

Miles is with us for the week while Janine is on vacation in the Cook Islands with her boyfriend. He wakes up every morning at 6 am, and comes downstairs to knock on my door and ask me to play with him and his kitten "Tigger". I've learned a trick to get a couple of hours more rest, which is to play a Walt Disney DVD and sleep on the couch beside him.

I wish Drew would take some more responsibility, but that doesn't seem likely to happen anytime soon. When he's not working at the computer on his nursing assignments, a glass of Cabernet Sauvignon within easy reach on his desk, he's in front of the TV watching rugby, or out with Bryce for a pint at the pub.

I looked at the calendar today, and realized that in ten months, I will be turning thirty and there is no boyfriend in sight, let alone a wedding on the horizon.

I made the mistake of picking up a copy of *Cosmopolitan* magazine today to read an article entitled, "Fertility Over Thirty: Should You Be Worried?" The short answer is yes, for the following reasons:

1. Men prefer younger women. This is a fact of life. If you are over thirty, you are already at a disadvantage because you should be wearing age-appropriate clothing, i.e., no hemlines above the knees. Most alpha males are visually aroused and appreciate a well-toned pair of legs in a thigh-grazing skirt. Unfortunately, if you're over the age of thirty and your name isn't Tina Turner, this option is out.

2. Your ovaries are not your best friends. If you are approaching thirty and you haven't had them frozen yet, you had better be on the phone making an appointment ASAP, otherwise, prepare yourself for a lifetime of childlessness. Repeat, prepare for a lifetime of no children.

3. Frankly, your chances of finding a man to marry you after the age of thirty are about the same as getting struck by lightening. No, wait—that's women over the age of forty. Frankly, your chances of finding a man to marry you after turning thirty are about the same as winning a million dollars in the lottery. In fact, they are slightly worse. So, you are probably better off spending your time buying lottery tickets so you can win the money you need to freeze your ovaries. At least then, you can have a child to comfort you in your old age, since you won't have a husband.

Sigh.
All in all, it's been a depressing day.

Affirmations
I am a strong, confident, capable woman
I wait in serene stillness, knowing my husband is on the way
If Oprah Winfrey can hear me now, I sincerely apologize.
I am no match for that woman and her ability to channel the powers
of the universe.

Kia Ora!
Kia Ora Nathan!
(That's Maori for hello.) I'm so sorry to hear you lost your job. I'm not
sure that getting fired for arriving late every day constitutes "unlawful
dismissal". But I'll check into it for you. Try not to feel depressed. On
the bright side, at least you can sleep in now. I've read over your questions
and I'll try my best to answer them. You should really just come and
visit.

Social Structure
The population here is just under four million spread across the
North and South Islands. The two main social groups are the "Maori"
(as you know), and the Pakeha (white descendants of the original British
settlers). I wouldn't describe the two groups as friendly. There are also
lots of people from the Pacific Islands and quite a few immigrants from
China and India.

Social Issues
• Ongoing land disputes between the Pakeha and Maori that are
  being heard under the Treaty of Waitangi.
• General animosity between the Pakeha and Maori that no one
  seems to admit openly, although my South African doctor told
  me the Kiwis would be happy if the Maori were all still riding
  at the back of the bus (!)
• Aucklanders are referred to as "Jaffas" outside of Auckland. It's
  a derogatory Maori expression. Don't ask me what it means.

Food
Similar to what Dad cooks at home.
Some typical meals:
Bangers and mash (sausages and mashed potatoes)

Fish and chips
Ham and cheese pie
Steak pie
Kumara (sweet potato/yam)
Bread pudding
Feijoas are in season right now. They're a green fruit that you can cut in half and eat with a spoon. They're supposed to have more vitamin C than oranges.

Culture

Sarcastic and repressed (except for Sydney who was raised by an unusually sexually liberated British mother and Kiwi father, now a senior partner at the oldest law firm in Wellington).

I don't think people generally like to be direct. They seem to clear their throats a lot and waggle their eyebrows meaningfully. It's different. Or as the Kiwis would say, "unusual".

Bryce is a good example of the conflicted feelings people have towards Americans (even though he's South African). He has a love/hate relationship with the United States. On one hand, he's always watching American programs on TV and listening to American music. On the other hand, Bryce is the first one to launch into criticism of North American politics and consumer culture, which is just plain hypocritical. But enough about him.

Tall Poppy Syndrome

This is one of the most interesting and confusing things about New Zealand culture. People don't like success, or at least, they don't like successful people who talk about their success. Sydney tried to explain this to me after I asked her why she thinks George (my International Languages professor), has been so hard on me. After making me promise not to ever quote her on anything, she told me that first of all, foreign students are only tolerated here because their tuition fees support the education system. So that was the first strike against me. Second, people hate Americans which is why there are hardly any here. No one will ever admit this to an American. Next, she thinks what really rankled George was when he asked everyone in our class to talk about our previous teaching experience. I talked about tutoring while I was going to university on exchange in Paris. This apparently made me a "tall poppy". She asked whether I know what "tall poppy syndrome" is, and I told her I have no idea. Withdrawal effects from smoking opium? She sighed, and told me to Google it. So I looked it up in Wikipedia, the free encyclopedia, which says:

Tall poppy syndrome (TPS) is a term used in Australasia for a leveling social attitude, pushed to the point of bad behavior. Someone has tall poppy syndrome when they are envious, defamatory, or overly critical of someone because of their notionally higher economic, social or political position.

Australians and New Zealanders have a reputation for resenting the success of others; whether this reputation is deserved or not is another question. Many Australasians have achieved success and wealth without attracting such hostility (e.g., Dick Smith). Apparent cases of tall poppy syndrome can often be explained as resentment not of success, but of snobbery and arrogance combined with an egalitarian attitude. Thus, Australians and New Zealanders are often self-deprecating, especially those in the public eye.

Another Definition
The tall poppy syndrome refers to the behavioural trait of Australians to cut down those who are 'superior' to them. It is used to explain why most politicians, some academics, and the occasional millionaire, command a level of community admiration inferior to that of a toilet cleaner.

And one more, posted on the internet by Bruce Kahl:
Tall poppy syndrome
If you tend to your garden and are successful in growing some flowers you will take the tallest, strongest specimen, cut it down and bring it indoors to be displayed.

It is also a tendency in some cultures to attack and "cut down" visibly successful people. As long as diversity of values exists, there will always be people criticizing those icons that are held up as the "model" that we should inspire to be like.

So, no wonder George hates me. I knew I shouldn't have talked so much about my traveling and exposure to French. Damn. Oh, well. It's too late now. Anyway, thank you for returning those *Sex And The City* DVDs for me. Say "hi" to Mom and Dad and good luck with your job hunt. I know you'll find something else, Big Brother.

Love,

Lindsay

Affirmations
This is the best year of my life
I am a brave, confident, capable woman
Every day, in every way,
I am less and less like a tall poppy

Chapter Two
Two Months Earlier...

I was sorting through some belongings tonight, when I came across my old diary from last year. I sat on the bed and flipped through the pages, stopping to read the entry I wrote on my twenty-ninth birthday.

Dear Diary,

Today I turned twenty-nine. It was an ordinary day, a work day, and it didn't turn out be a great one despite waking up early to do yoga and meditate. I also ate an antioxidant-rich, low fat breakfast (unfortunately, it left me so hungry that as soon as I got to the subway station, I ran to the bakery and bought two cream cheese danishes. The danishes made me happy for about five minutes. Then, I realized I had blown my first resolution on my list of goals for "My 29th Year": Avoiding fats and sweets for breakfast). The morning was cold and rainy, which didn't seem to bode well for my last 365 days before turning the big "0." In fact, I seem to be having some kind of "pre-0" meltdown. I can't even write out the "three" Okay, there I just did. Progress! Well, sort of.

I was late for work and of course, the second resolution on my list was to "Establish a new and healthy pattern of punctual behavior for the year". In all honesty, there was no way of knowing that my meticulous plans from the night before would go so horribly awry. I had bought a brand new pair of pantyhose, to wear with my new wool skirt and new shoes. As soon as I put my first leg in, I saw a telltale sliver of bare skin beginning at my ankle, widening into a full- fledged run that continued all the way up my thigh. I think I was in denial because I sat on my bed staring at the run for a good ten minutes, trying to convince myself that it wasn't really that noticeable. I didn't have time to do laundry this week, so there were no backup pairs available. I started to panic, and then remembered reading an article somewhere that said bare legs are more acceptable if they're tanned. I grabbed a bottle of "auto bronzer" from under the bathroom sink. It only took a few minutes to apply, and since I was determined to wear my new skirt on my birthday, it seemed like a good solution. It was a mistake. As soon as she got to the office, Hazel, one of the partners, pounced on me.

"Lindsay! Do you know what time it is? We have a client meeting in fifteen minutes!"

I glanced at my watch with a sinking feeling in the pit of my stomach: It was already fifteen minutes past 9 am.

"I'm sorry. It's one of those days. Actually, it's my birthday," I said, smiling hopefully.

"Congratulations. I want to see that client's file updated and on my desk in five minutes."

She turned to leave, and I breathed as sigh of relief, thinking I was off the hook. Unfortunately, my computer alarm then went off, reminding me that I had a client meeting in fifteen minutes. Hazel's eyes were drawn to the monitor, where my *Us Magazine* screensaver was running. Her brow furrowed as she looked at the photos of insipidly beaming celebrities on my monitor. Then, her glance fell to my collection of magazines that I keep in a rack beside my desk, and travelled down to my bare legs, which weren't as well shaven as I seemed to remember. Horse-like features darkening into a scowl, she walked over to shut my office door.

"Sit down, Lindsay."

Damn.

"I'd like to ask you something." She took a seat in the chair in front of me, studying me for a few moments like a beady-eyed hawk. I glanced downwards, and suddenly noticed my knuckles, which were tangerine orange. Damn! I had forgotten to wash my hands after applying the auto-bronzer. The insides of my fingers resembled those of a primate, making me feel like an orangutan trapped inside a corporate, glass-plated menagerie. I quickly hid my hands in my lap.

"Do you think you're a serious person?" Hazel asked.

"Yes."

"Serious about your work here?"

"Yes."

"Serious about arriving on time in the morning?"

I squirmed in my seat, silently praying for an interruption. Our receptionist, Colleen, usually called by this time to ask if I wanted a coffee from downstairs. Where was she? How did I get trapped behind a closed door with Hazel, who seems to derive her only pleasure in life by making mine miserable? She recently had white skunk stripes added to her jet-black hair. Now she looks like Cruella De Vil from the movie *101 Dalmatians* and she has a personality to match. Not that most lawyers in this office are particularly nice. Why did I ever go into law in the first place? Oh, that's right. It seemed like a good idea at the time because I didn't know what else to do with my life. I stared at the phone. Ring phone, ring.

"...dressing appropriately? Answer me!"

"I'm sorry?"

I had no idea what Cruella had just said, but I doubted it would contribute to my emotional well-being. At a moment like this, what would Tony Robbins do? I've been reading his book, *Awaken the Giant Within*, which promises to teach me how to "Take immediate control of your mental, emotional, physical and financial destiny!" Chapter Sixteen says, "Nothing has to happen in order for you to feel good." According to Tony, I should be able to feel good right now, for no reason whatsoever! I had reviewed the chapter on the subway and it said that as I start each day, I should make a rule that I'm going to enjoy it no matter what happens. So much for that theory.

Riiing!

Thank God, it must be Colleen, I thought.

"Excuse me," I said to Hazel, who was now standing with her arms folded across her chest, nostrils flaring like a filly about to throw its rider from the saddle.

"Hello?"

"Happy birthday, Sunshine!"

Oh my God! Ben!

"Oh my God! Ben!" I croaked into the phone.

"How ya do'in, Cutie? Survivin' the corporate jungle?"

"Umm…"

I glanced over at Hazel who was staring at me pointedly, waiting for me to hurry up and get off the phone.

"Not really. We're just about to go into a client meeting."

"That's OK, just wanted to wish you happy birthday. I've got some news."

My heart started pounding in my chest, even though I had no idea what he was going to say.

"What is it?"

Hazel was now drumming her fingernails on my desk, eyes boring into me as though mentally envisioning a karate kick to my solar plexus. According to Colleen, she wakes up every morning at 5 am to take Tai Bo lessons and "visualize" her day.

"Well…"

A loud knock came at the door, and Hazel abruptly turned to answer it. It was Jeff, one of the other partners. He glanced at me, then at Hazel, with an inquisitive eyebrow raised. She shook her head and motioned for him to step back into the hall, then followed him, slamming the door shut with a reverberating bang.

"What was that?" asked Ben.

"Cruella."

"Who?"

"Never mind. Ben, I'm sorry. I can't talk right now."

"No sweat. Call me tonight, 'K?"

"OK. Bye."

"Bye."

I replaced the receiver, sat back in my desk, and listened to the rain drum heavily against the window. That's when I realized, with slowly growing horror, that in my haste to catch the bus this morning, I had forgotten my old brief case by the door. After waking up, I had emptied the contents of my old purse into my new handbag, but not the contents of my briefcase. Which is where the client file was, that I had spent three hours working on from 10 pm until 1 am in the morning.

***

By four o'clock this afternoon, I was more than ready to come home. Hazel didn't let me take lunch, amongst other ghoulish punishments for not remembering to bring our client's file. (As it turned out, the client got held up at another meeting and never did make it for his appointment, but the damage was already done.) After ordering me to do her assistant's filing, make hundreds of photocopies, and wash her coffee cup in the sink, Hazel spent a good half-hour lecturing me in her office while the support staff murmured sympathetically on the other side of the door. She questioned whether I'm really committed to the firm, and wondered aloud about my lack of organizational skills and questionable intelligence: "Well, you finished law school, so you can't be a complete idiot," she mused uncharitably.

I was beside myself, and wondered what terrible thing I had done in a past life, that was now coming back to haunt me. Not that I believe in past lives, but I can't think of any other explanation for my hellish working conditions. According to Colleen, Hazel burns through junior associates faster than a heavy smoker finishes a pack of cigarettes. Her spitefulness hasn't won her too many fans at the office, but since she brings in a large volume of clients, the other partners turn a blind eye to it. Had I known what I was getting into, I would have declined this position and taken the less well-paid job I was offered with the United Way. It probably serves me right for choosing profit over charity.

I finally left the office at 7 pm, which is early for our firm, but I didn't have the heart to work anymore. After cashing my pay check at the bank, I started to head towards the subway home, and noticed a new issue of *Elle Magazine* on the newsstand. I impulsively decided to flip through it, and found an article on "Age Appropriate" clothing. I read in dismay as the *Elle* writer waxed poetic about the rhapsodies of youth, and the ability of the twenty-something to get away with "Fun, sexy, adventurous clothing—now is the time to experiment!" The thirty-something year-old, on the other hand, is advised to, "Choose clothes that reflect your maturity and sophistication". Oh my God! I'm only 365 days away from being forced into cutting my hair and donating all my mini-skirts to the United Way!

I practically flew up the escalator and out the door, heading towards Queen Street where I'd be sure to find lots of "Fun, sexy and adventurous" clothing. And then it dawned on me: this is it. I've just turned twenty nine, and I'm supposed to have accomplished a lot more than working at a miserable position that barely covers my exorbitant rent and student loan interest payments. I'm the last of my girlfriends from high school not to be married. I'm the only one renting an apartment and eating frozen dinners in front of the TV every night. So, if I'm going to be single, I should make the most of it, shouldn't I? Now's the time to date and have all the crazy adventures you're supposed to leave behind after saying "I do".

As these thoughts were going through my head, I turned the corner and passed by the University of Toronto Campus. There was a large banner across the doors of the Education Building that said, "Study Abroad—Recruitment Night". I stopped for a moment, looked at my watch and thought, *what the heck?*

***

Three hours later, I was in the shower shaving my legs when the phone rang. I hurried out of the bathroom, a large, bleach-stained towel wrapped around me.

"Hello?" I answered, dripping water into the telephone receiver.

"Hi Sunshine!"

Ben! I had totally forgotten about him.

"Hey! How's it goin'?"

"Great! How are you?"

"Good, good."

There was an awkward silence and I wondered why he was calling me. It was just over eight months since we had broken up. Correction. Since he had broken up with me, claiming that he needed to focus on his career. He knew that I was looking for a commitment, which I thought was reasonable after four years together, but apparently not. According to Ben's logic, it made more sense to wait a couple of years until things were more financially "stable". He had assured me that he still loved me, but needed time for himself to "get things on the right track". Down the road, he said, who knew what the future would hold? I felt a small glimmer of hope flicker inside me. Was he calling to get back together? What would I say? Could I really take him back?

"Hey...what was the news you had for me this morning?" I asked.

"You'll never guess...I'm getting married!"

"You're...*WHAT?*" I was sure I had misunderstood him.

"I'm getting married, Lindsay! I wanted you to be the first to know!"

"But...I didn't even know you were dating anybody!"

"It hasn't been long. Four months. But she's amazing, Lindz. She's got her Masters in English...I mean, she's really smart. I can barely keep up with her! She's just got this incredible intellect, she's funny, she's laid back, she's beautiful. I mean, she has a shit-hot body..."

"I get the picture," I said quickly.

"Ben, I have to go." I could feel my nose burning, which meant that tears were on their way. The last thing I wanted to do was cry on the phone while my ex-boyfriend listened.

"What do you mean you have to go?"

"This is—what happened to waiting two years until things are financially stable?"

"Lindsay I'm in love! I thought you'd be happy for me."

"So, you weren't in love with me?"

"What? You know I still love you. We just aren't meant to be together for the long run."

"You know, it's been a really long day. I should get going."

"Lindz, what's going on with you?"

"Nothing's going on with me! It's just my birthday, and I'm twenty nine...I only have a year left to wear fun clothes. I hate my job and nothing makes sense to me anymore!"

I started crying.

"Sweetie—you don't still have feelings for me, do you?"

"No, I don't! Don't flatter yourself!"

"I'm not."

There were a few moments of heavy silence on his end, and muffled sobs on mine. Finally, he said, "OK Lindsay, I'm going to let you go."

"OK."

"Can I call you later?"

"Ben? Can you do something for me?"

"Sure, what is it?"

"Don't ever call me again."

I hung up the phone and spent the rest of the night crying my eyes out on the couch. I also managed to devour an entire carton of Haagen Daaz triple brownie ice cream and three orange cream vodka coolers. My Aunt Dorothy called from England at midnight, to wish me a happy birthday and ask whether I've got myself "a bloke" yet. I told her that I was taking an indefinite break from men, quitting my job, and moving to New Zealand.

"Still a spinster," she sighed. Apparently the part about quitting my job and moving to the other side of the world had gone right over her head.

"Auntie D, did you hear me? I'm quitting my job and moving to New Zealand next year!"

"You're what?"

"The University had a "study abroad" exhibition tonight. I can do teaching training in New Zealand and get to spend the whole year sightseeing! The recruiter says that teacher's college is a piece of cake, and I'll have the time of my life there!"

"You'll have what?"

The line started to crackle and I realized she was having trouble hearing me.

"It's going to be the adventure of a lifetime!" I yelled into the receiver.

"Don't worry, Lindsay love. You'll find someone. Now you have a nice birthday drink for me. Be good to yourself, lass! Ta-rah! Bye!"

"Bye Auntie D. Thanks for calling."

I wondered whether my Aunt Dorothy had had a few "birthday" drinks of her own.

It didn't matter. I had just made the most important decision of my life. I was going to quit my job and move to New Zealand to study at teacher's college. If that doesn't "awaken the giant within," I don't know what will.

I crawled into bed, looking up at my bedroom ceiling decorated with glow-in-the-dark stickers representing the solar system. I was finally taking control of my destiny, making life happen instead of letting life happen to me. Onward and upward…

I felt myself begin to drift into a peaceful if slightly boozy sleep, and reached over to switch off my reading light where my list of resolutions for "My 29th Year," were taped to the wall:

1. *I will avoid all fats and sweets for breakfast.*
   (Strike one, I had those two cream cheese danishes this morning)
2. *I will establish a healthy pattern of punctual behavior.*
   (Strike two)
3. *I will make important decisions carefully, weighing pros and cons before acting.*
   (This resolution was to remedy what my parents call, my "tendency to be impulsive")

Well, maybe some well-timed impulsivity now and then can be a good thing...

Chapter Three
February

Some Girls Are Born Winners

My Christian Dior sweater is soaking in a bucket of Kiwi "washing powder" that Drew promises will make the pink go away. I hope he's right. Doing laundry is something of an adventure here. I've noticed that now both Drew and Bryce have been leaving their wet laundry in the washer, so I end up hanging it up outside for them so that I can get my own clothes washed. I feel self-conscious about my "holey" underwear so I try to hang them between the towels and bed sheets at the far end of the clothesline, which just makes them laugh while they watch me from the kitchen window. Tigger, our calico kitten, likes watching while I work as well, and attacks the clothes on the line with her claws, which has resulted in several shredded pairs of pantyhose.

Drew has continued leaving the toilet seat up, something he didn't do before Bryce moved in. Every time I use the bathroom, I slam the seat down to make a point, but I'm not sure that anyone is really paying attention. I almost wish that Helena were still here so I'd have another woman around for moral support.

Drew confessed he was feeling blue the other day, because he doesn't think he's doing a great job of being a single father. It was hard not to agree, but I kept silent and made him a cup of green tea, which seemed to make him feel better.

"You know what I do when I need some extra confidence?"

"What?"

"I wear my 'Juicy Couture' T-shirt. Honestly, it works every time. I was wearing it when I flew into L.A., and it was the first time in my life that I didn't have any problems at customs."

"Your juicy *what* T-shirt?"

"My *Juicy Couture* T-shirt. You know, the one that says 'Some Girls are Born Winners' on the front?"

"Isn't that the one that says 'Juicy' across your chest? I reckon I'd let you through customs too."

Damn! This could explain a lot. I had changed out of that T-shirt into my Guess? sweater after I got to LAX which is when the quality of service I had been receiving suddenly changed as well.

The next day, Drew came home with three new shirts, and asked if I could "keep an eye" on Miles while he went for a pint with Bryce. He also asked me not to use the dryer this week because household expenses were getting too high. Given that Drew is from a multimillionaire family, he shouldn't have trouble affording anything, but apparently Helena is trying to teach him a lesson, and the Bank of Mom is officially closed for business. This has done nothing to change his expensive tastes, however. I noticed that one of his new shirts has a "Hugo Boss" label. I promised myself to think twice the next time I feel the impulse to give advice.

This afternoon, Drew came to pick me up from school with Miles. Bryce was waiting at the house to help move a wardrobe from the garage into my bedroom. Drew discovered it when he moved in last year, and has since painted white over the scratched oak. Unfortunately, it doesn't seem that he gave much thought as to whether or not it would actually fit through the doors in the house. After the two guys had spent about ten minutes huffing and puffing, Drew finally said, "Hey, Bryce, do you have some elastic to tie the doors shut? Lindsay, do you have a hair band?"

I quickly retrieved a pink fishnet scarf and tried to tie the doors together.

"I don't think it's the right..."

"Color?" interrupted Bryce, sarcastically.

(I was going to say "size".)

More huffing and puffing ensued while I watched helplessly. A few minutes turned into two hours. Bryce had wanted to go to the pub to watch rugby with his mates and Drew seemed oblivious to his frustration. At one point he said,

"Shivers! I really wish I'd a' thought of the dimensions of the room earlier."

To which Bryce dryly responded,

"Yeah. I wish I'd a'…Left. An hour ago."

Drew told Bryce to go ahead to the pub and the wardrobe was left in the garage. We then made our way to my room to measure the doorframe. Miles, who had been napping, woke up and started to cry. I saw Drew's gaze shift to the window where Bryce was climbing into an old green Volvo that looked like it had about seven passengers packed inside.

Not again, I thought.

"Hey Drew, thanks so much for trying to move the wardrobe for me. I've got a barbecue tonight, so I'm going to start getting ready now."

Miles suddenly appeared at the bedroom door.

"Can I come to the barbecue, Lindsay? Please Daddy, can I go to the barbecue?"

Drew looked at me hopefully, and I quickly tried to think of an excuse.

Thankfully, I didn't have to stall for very long because the phone rang and it was Janine on the other end of the line. I grabbed my toiletry bag and headed into the bathroom, locking the door behind me. Pulling back the lemon yellow curtains, I had a clear view of the backyard. Drew's navy Hugo Boss shirt was hanging on the line, along with Miles' red corduroy overalls, Bryce's jeans, and two of my faded, fuchsia-streaked pairs of underwear. In the far left corner of the yard, an orange tree was beginning to bear fruit. The rest of the yard was mostly taken up by a lopsided blue and yellow swing set that Drew had installed for Miles. As the sun set across a sleepy sky embroidered with swirls of pink and gold, it cast long shadows on Drew's overgrown lawn. The air outside was warm and the breeze carried the sound of Helena's wind chimes, which she had tied to a lower bough on the orange tree.

I reached down to turn on the bathtub faucets, and could hear Drew scolding Miles, who started to cry again. Ten minutes later when I finished my shower, I heard Miles' little hand steadily knocking on the door. I quickly wrapped myself in a worn purple beach towel, then opened it. Miles was standing before me, face streaked with tears, holding a scruffy Paddington Bear tightly in one arm.

"Lindsay!" he exclaimed joyfully, his face lighting up as he threw his arms around my waist.

I immediately felt a twinge of guilt. I would have rescued him sooner but I had been trying to shave my legs as quickly as I could without slipping in the tub. I made a mental note to ask Drew to buy a safety mat before I have a serious mishap.

Miles quickly made himself at home inside the bathroom, followed by Tigger who jumped on the side of the bathtub, tail swishing as she licked the droplets of water she found.

"What's this Lindsay?" asked Miles, holding up an amber-coloured blush set.

"That, is a blush brush. Can you say blush brush?"

"Blush!" he repeated, giggling.

"Good! You are a clever boy!"

" I are!"

"You are!"

"And what's this Lindsay?"

"That is a nail clipper. You use it to clip your nails."

"Can you...clip my nails Lindsay?"

"Not now, Sweetheart. Maybe your Daddy can clip your nails tonight."

(There was a loud sneeze from the other side of the bathroom door and I realized that "Daddy" was eavesdropping.)

"What's this? What's this for?"

Miles, beginning to enjoy the game, was gleefully waving a tampon he had found in my cosmetic bag. I heard another loud sneeze. Clearly, Drew was not making the most of his time to get ahead with his nursing assignment.

"Tha—at is...for ladies. Can you pretend to comb your hair with Lindsay?"

And fifteen minutes later, I found myself unwittingly babysitting once again, holding Miles on my lap in front of the TV while Drew argued on the phone with Janine, who had called back again.

"I am the best thing that ever happened to you!" she had screamed over the phone one night while Drew insisted I listen. I sincerely hoped she was wrong, because it didn't say much for the quality of the man's life. That was the night of the Great Toaster Negotiation, to which Bryce and I were both unfortunate witnesses. (The negotiation involved a prolonged dispute over the ownership of a toaster that The Best Thing That Ever Happened wanted back.)

By the time I arrived at the barbecue it was close to 9 pm, and most of the guests had already eaten. Sydney was in all of her glory as hostess, green eyes sparkling, wavy auburn hair pulled back into an elegant chignon at the nape of her neck. She reminded me of a butterfly, flitting from one room to the next in a flowing white sundress that showed off her summer tan. After quickly kissing me on the cheek and taking my jacket from me, she disappeared into the kitchen, and reappeared with a glass of Chardonnay that she pressed into my hand.

"Make yourself at home, Lindsay. So glad you could make it. Lots of yummy blokes here," she winked, before disappearing through the patio doors to tend to her guests outside.

Before I could take a sip of my wine, I was accosted by an aggressive man from Dubai that I recognized from my old social studies class. He kept leering at me, while trying to find out the fastest way to immigrate to Canada. Looking around the room for an escape, I spotted a couple with two small children eating feijoas at the kitchen table. I excused myself and joined them, thinking I would be safe from the unwanted male attention. I was wrong.

The husband, who was peeling feijoas with a paring knife, looked at me lustfully from across the table and said, "I don't believe you're at Tutage Teacher's College. I would have remembered meeting such a gorgeous woman. Isn't she gorgeous Lydia?"

"Yes, gorgeous," his wife said coldly, looking as though she wanted to grab the knife out of his hands and stab him with it.

"Look at the lashes on those big, brown eyes, and those gorgeous curls. Why don't you do your hair like that Lydia?"

"Oh, I don't know Richard. Why don't you stop being such an arse?"

I quickly excused myself and went to use the phone in Sydney's bedroom at the end of the hall. The walls were painted soft peach, framed by a floral border with matching bishop sleeve curtains. A queen-sized bed was covered by a praline silk duvet, and her walnut vanity table had a tidy collection of perfume and make-up neatly arranged by the mirror, where a cordless phone stood. I took the phone and sat down on a cream-colored leather couch by the window, placing my wine on the glass coffee table in front of me.

"Hey, Drew! How would you like to join me at the barbecue? I know Miles wanted to come."

"A bun-fight? Sweet-as!"

"Um…I take it that means *yes?*"

Drew was clearly happy to get the invitation and arrived shortly afterwards with Miles, who ran to throw himself in my arms when he saw me. Miles led me into the living room where Richard and Lydia's children were busy doing summersaults. Drew quickly got himself a beer and settled in front of the TV to watch the rugby match. Lydia's little girl, dressed in a pink tutu and sparkly tiara, was eager to show me the curtseys she had learned from her ballet teacher. I noticed that Miles had already found time to scribble on Sydney's wall with a pen and wondered whether to say anything to Sydney, then thought better of it.

Glancing out the window, I saw Sydney in her garden. She was laughing as she spoke to a tall man who reached over to pick an apricot rose from the bushes behind her, and place it in her hair. He turned sideways for a moment and I realized it was Bryce! I didn't think he and Sydney knew each other, but since we're all in the same program, it makes sense. He must have finished early at the pub.

For a moment, I tried to see Bryce through Sydney's eyes. Despite being gangly, I could see how girls would think he's cute with his mop of curly brown hair, twinkling hazel eyes and impish grin. He was wearing a navy blue and white striped polo shirt, white shorts and sports sandals, Oakley sunglasses perched on top of his head. He and Sydney seemed to be in a world of their own, and for just a moment, I envied them.

***

Two hours later, after saying an awkward goodbye to Richard and Lydia, who dryly thanked me for baby-sitting their children, I bundled Miles into the car, strapping him into the child seat in the back, where he fell asleep with his Paddington Bear tucked beside him. Drew joined me, having finally pried himself away from the TV, and we headed home. On the way, Drew asked whether I'm familiar with the Southern constellation, and when I said no, he headed towards the marina down the road from his house. We parked by the dock, sunroof and windows open so we could enjoy the warm breeze.

The sky was filled with hundreds of stars shining like beaded crystals sewn to midnight-blue velvet. I glanced over at Drew who was gazing out at the water, one muscular, tanned arm on the steering wheel, the other draped over the open car window. His strong jaw line was marred only by a small, jagged scar that ended just under his chin. The air was filled with the woodsy scent of his cologne, and the only sound besides the lapping waves was Miles softly snoring in the back seat.

"Drew, thanks for trying to move the wardrobe for me today."

"That's OK, Lindsay. He turned to face me and smiled.

"Which constellations do you recognize?"

"None of them."

"Here." He took my hand and pointed it towards a cluster of stars to our right.

"That's the Southern Cross."

I could feel Drew's breath hot against my neck, and didn't trust myself to look at him.

The last time I had been this physically close to a man was a year earlier when Ben took me to the beach one night while we were living on the West Coast. Since we had shared our first kiss at the beach, I thought he had brought me there to propose. As it turned out, it was the opposite. He wanted to break up with me. At that moment, my entire world was turned upside down. I've never felt as though it's been quite the same, since. Ben was the man I thought I was going to spend the rest of my life with. I left behind family and friends to move 3,000 miles away from home to be with him, and the four years we'd spent together were the happiest ones of my life. Who would have thought I would leave the West Coast for Toronto, only to discover that law isn't for me after all? And who would have thought I'd then impulsively decide to move to the other side of the world?

Tonight's Affirmations
This is the best year of my life
I believe in miracles, and I now welcome their manifesting
I wait in serene stillness, knowing my husband is the on the way

A Class Act

The Tutage international student recruiter that my father would like me to sue (in addition to the Tutage Teacher's College) was right about one thing: there is no doubt whatsoever that my trip to New Zealand has been an adventure of a lifetime.

My first practicum placement as a student teacher was at Papakura College, a "decile one school" with a mainly Pacific Islander population. Marion, my former social studies lecturer, had insisted that students from the Pacific Islands were all warm and friendly, and made it sound like teaching them would be a piece of cake (or as Bryce would say, "a piece of piss").

The first indication this would not be the case came after I discovered the true meaning of a "decile one" school. In New Zealand, schools are ranked from one to ten, and those at the low end of the scale are located in "resource challenged" neighborhoods which means that you're basically teaching at an inner-city school that should have metal detectors but doesn't.

My practicum at Papakura College was a spectacular failure. For some reason, I was assigned to a grade twelve physics class, even though I was supposed to be teaching French. To say that I'm terrified of math and science would be an understatement. How I ever passed the accounting portion of my bar exams, I'll never know. It was like a divine miracle of God.

I watched as the mainly Pacific Island students filed into the classroom and wrote the word "TALL" in my observation notes.

"Miss! Miss! You're looking very nice today, Miss!" I heard someone say.

"Nice tits!" yelled someone else from the back of the classroom.

I sank down in my seat and wished I had never boarded that plane in Toronto.

"You have filthy minds," screamed the East Indian physics teacher, who was standing at the front of the classroom, hair dishevelled, glasses askew, green polyester sari covered in chalk dust. This only had the effect of eliciting more rude comments and obscene gestures, while the physics teacher continued to scream at the students to shut their mouths, and broke chalk stick after chalk stick against the blackboard. After ten minutes, she finally tired of screaming and said,

"Miss! Would you come to the front of the classroom please?'

"Me?" I stared at her.

"Yes. Come to the front of the classroom please. I'd like you to say something."

"What would you like me to say?"

"Say anything—just teach the lesson," she said, before disappearing through the door, leaving me to stand in front of a classroom full of seventeen year olds with absolutely nothing to say. I wondered whether she planned to come back.

The students were all staring at me and I felt a sudden urge to disappear myself.

"Uh...So, does anyone have any questions about Canada?"

To my surprise nearly everyone raised their hands, but my impromptu lesson was hijacked when a fight broke out at the back of the classroom. Two rival gang members were promising to "beat the shit" out of each other while the students divided into two groups on either side of the classroom, yelling "Fight! Fight!" I had no idea what to do, and ran to ask for help from the teacher next door.

Half an hour later, I was in the guidance office trying to explain how I came to be left alone on my first day of teaching observations, which is strictly against regulations. This led to a meeting with the Principal, Vivienne, who told me I had failed to observe proper protocol because I went to another teacher for assistance instead of reporting directly to her. I tried to explain that in the heat of the moment, I did the first thing that seemed logical. I also pointed out that her office is on the other side of the school and besides, I have a terrible sense of direction and might have spent the rest of the morning wandering through the corridors.

"You like to talk a lot, don't you?" she snapped, glaring at me from across her desk while tapping a long, red fingernail against a sheaf of papers in front of her. Her cold blue eyes made the hair stand on the back of my neck.

"Well, I did used to be a lawyer."

She looked even more unhappy, if that was possible. Her lipstick was the color of dried cranberries, and bled into the tiny wrinkles around her mouth, which was turned downward into a frown.

"The college didn't prepare you very well," she said crisply.

"Can you explain to me why it's necessary to see a visiting lecturer tomorrow? You should be in the classroom."

I had no idea why I had to see a visiting lecturer the next day.

"Well, umm…honestly no, I can't really explain."

"I see." She wrote something down on the top sheet in front of her, then briskly folded it and placed it into an envelope marked "Confidential".

"That will be all, thank you."

"Thanks."

Later, I saw the evaluation she had given me, and felt my first serious twinge of doubt about my ability to successfully complete my academic year.

Student Name: Lindsay Breyer

School: Papakura College

Coordinator: Vivienne Jones

Learning Outcomes: **LOs Achieved**
LO1
Demonstrates a developing understanding of the complexity
and constraints of secondary school environments.   NO.
LO2
Demonstrates professionalism.   NO.

Comments to Support Decision:

Did not use correct channels when confronted with problems.

Was a negative influence on other Tutage students in her attempt to be their advocate.

Further Comment (if any):

I believe that Lindsay needs to seriously consider the wisdom of pursuing teaching as a career path.

* * *

Attempt to be an advocate? All I did was ask if the student teachers could use the microwave to heat our lunches in the staff room. Sydney wasn't joking when she said they give foreign students a hard time here.

My father was horrified when I told him what happened, and he demanded that I either file a complaint with the Principal of Tutage Teacher's College, or sue them for a refund.

Could I really be that bad? And why does everyone I meet seem to hate me?

I have to start doing more affirmations and rebuild my self-confidence.

Affirmations
I am a strong, confident, capable woman
I am invincible
I am an academic legend

More Misgivings About Middle Earth

The neighbourhood where Drew lives, Onetai, is a mainly working class suburb that gradually deteriorates into a ghetto as you venture further south. Motorcycle gangs are out on the weekend as police helicopters patrol the city and/or chase criminals. I've tried telling my friends at teacher's college that we don't have quite the same social problems in Canada. There aren't any helicopters chasing down drug lords on Toronto city streets. Still, they've been skeptical.

"Honestly. Honest to God. There are no police helicopters out on the weekend. I swear."

"Good country, Canada. Didn't you say your table syrup comes out of trees?" asked Jordy, with a snicker.

"Why do you think it's called *maple* syrup? Oh, never mind."

I gave up.

Talking to my friends at home was worse.

"So, Lindsay! How's everything going? Are you taking lots of pictures?"

"Not really. Did you know that Auckland has the highest rate of teenage suicide in the world? And there's this drug called "P" that's a huge problem with teenagers, it's an amphetamine they smuggle from the Pacific Islands. And they actually have helicopters chasing down criminals on the weekend!"

"In New Zealand? That doesn't sound right."

"I'm telling you, it is *not* like *Lord of the Rings*! And there's this crazy woman who keeps threatening to chop my hair off, Drew's ex-wife. Hello? Hello?"

If it weren't for Peter Jackson and his *Lord of the Rings* trilogy, I would be sitting in my office on Bay Street right now, looking at the newest Guess? catalogue instead of freezing to death every night because there's no central heating at Drew's house.

So much for vacationing on a tropical island for a year. I should sue for false advertising.

Helpful Affirmations
I am willing to see things differently
I am willing to forgive Peter Jackson
I am comfortably and easily adapting to life in New Zealand

The Best Thing That Ever Happened
Janine has been leaving an alarming number of messages on the voice mail for the past few days, including promises to "drive out all of the flatmates, drive that American tart straight back to Canada," and make (our) lives hell because we have to pay for the consequences of her decision. What decision, I have no idea. I don't know how I end up in these situations.

"Lindsay," my mother whispered on the phone last night. "I think you should come home."

"Why are you whispering Mom?"

"I don't want to wake up your father. Does the school know about the situation?"

"Not yet."

"I think you should come home, dear. We don't want anything to happen to you."

"I'll be fine, I promise."

"I'm going to call the Canadian Consulate in the morning."

"What? No!"

"Lindsay, I don't think you're taking this seriously. I'll have your father call you tomorrow."

"Oh, no! Mom, don't!"

"Will you talk to Nathan, then?"

"Mom, please. Look, I promise I'll go back to Beatrice and talk to her about it."

"I thought you said you don't want to go back to Beatrice?"

"Mom, this is ridiculous. You worry too much!"

"If anything happens, call 911. And I want you to phone here anytime if you need to, day or night. We'll send Nathan to come and get you."

"I'll be fine."

"Please be careful, Lindsay. Is there anywhere you can buy a can of pepper spray?"

"Mom! I'll be fine. I'll talk to Drew, I promise. Bye!"

Thankfully, my mother was not privy to the conversation I ended up having with Drew, which went something like this:

"Hey Drew?"

"Yup?"

"I'm getting a bit worried about Janine's phone calls."

"Oh, I wouldn't worry about her."

"Well, my family at home is pretty concerned—I don't want her coming here to confront me, or whatever."

"She won't come here."

"But what if she does? Shouldn't we have a plan?"

"She won't. Trust me."

Today's Morning Affirmations
I am a strong, confident, capable woman
I am not afraid of Drew's ex-wife

***

This afternoon I helped Drew with his nursing assignment, which he was handing in past the deadline. Drew handwrites all of his assignments before typing out his notes, and I told him this isn't the most time-efficient way of doing things. Since I have Fridays off, I agreed to type his notes for him, and proofread his work just this once.

We were nearing his five o'clock deadline, when we both heard a car pull up in the driveway. It was Janine. I locked myself in my bedroom, anxious to avoid an unpleasant domestic scene. Slipping on a pair of earplugs, I tried to focus on my psychology reading and ignore the raised voices. I thought I heard the word "toaster" and for a moment, was grateful for being single.

Finally, hunger drove me out to the kitchen, where Janine was standing by the window. Skinny as a shoestring liquorice, she stood at least six feet tall, with shiny black bobbed hair, heavy eye makeup and a nose ring. She was wearing a torn black T-shirt and black denim, with black, high heel leather boots. Bryce, who had ventured into the kitchen for a cup of coffee, looked terrified of her. I was surprised that Drew had married someone who towered over him like a gothic Amazon.

As I tried to feign nonchalance in the kitchen and focus on making myself a tuna sandwich, Janine stood quietly, watching me with a deranged smile on her face. She then sat down at the kitchen table, took an emery board out of her purse, and starting filing her nails.

I felt annoyed with myself for feeling intimidated in my own kitchen. Who did this Kiwi woman think she was, dropping by unannounced and sitting in my chair?

"You know, Janine," I said, trying to ignore the tremor in my voice, "You really should have rang before coming by. I don't have anything to offer you to eat."

"That's quite alright. I really feel quite comfortable here."

"Well, if you ring next time before coming 'round, I can make sure to have some tea and biscuits."

I hoped that I sounded breezy and nonchalant but my heart was pounding and I wondered why I was using words like "ring" and "biscuits".

"I'm really quite comfortable," she smiled.

At least someone was.

Drew was sitting on the loveseat looking shell-shocked. Not seeing a happy ending to the entire scenario, I told that him that I was going to Sydney's and he immediately offered to drive me. The trouble was, he had already promised Bryce a ride to the ferry because he was going home for the weekend (Bryce's family live on an island off the coast and he often goes back on Friday nights). Janine then stood up and announced that she would give Bryce a ride, causing him to turn a deathly shade of white. I wondered whether Drew's life was always this dramatic. Time would tell.

Tonight's Affirmations
I am comfortably and easily adapting to Kiwi life
(even though I'd rather be at home)
I am a grounded and confident woman
I wait in serene stillness, knowing my husband is on the way

MEN ARE LIKE MOCHA LATTES

***

Mr. Henry Whittaker
Principal,
Tutage Teacher's College

Dear Henry,

I am writing to inform you of some concerns that I've had since being recruited to study at Tutage Teacher's College.

First, someone might have warned me about the deadly pollen here. I have had severe allergic reactions to your country's plants and flowers, and feel you have breached a serious duty to warn of this danger.

Second, while still in Canada I took your Housing Director's advice to share accommodation with "Drew" in Onetai. You may be interested to know that we do not have ghettos such as Onetai at home where the standard of living is much higher and far superior to New Zealand.

As someone who worked one summer for the Canadian Government in diplomatic relations, I should also tell you that your college staff could use some training in cultural sensitivity. I do not appreciate being called an "American" by lecturers and am deeply offended by same. Nor do I appreciate being daily threatened and harassed by a jealous, local Kiwi woman, and certainly not by the jealous ex-wife of my flatmate, a situation of which you were aware, or ought to have been aware of prior to placing my life in this danger.

I would appreciate your prompt attention to these matters, and take this opportunity to remind you that I am a lawyer.

I remain yours faithfully, etc.,
Lindsay Breyer

A Proper Thumping

I've been nursing a headache all day after my first "girls' night out" in New Zealand. When I told Sydney what happened with Vivienne at Papakura College, she insisted on taking me for a night on the town to get my mind off everything. Drowning my sorrows in alcohol seemed like a good idea at the time, so I agreed, not realizing I would end up with the worst hangover of my life.

Sydney came to pick me up in her red Mazda Miata, top down, her "Pink" CD cranked up to full volume on the stereo. I could see she had more than drinking on her mind for the evening, dressed in a tight black halter top with no bra, black mini skirt, and four inch spiked heels. Her hair was slicked back in a high pony tail, lips painted bright red, eyelids darkened with kohl.

She raised an eyebrow as I got in the passenger seat beside her, taking in my plain white T-shirt, faded jeans and sandals.

"Lindsay, did you think we were going for a picnic at the beach?"

"Very funny."

"Honestly, you'll never catch a bloke dressed like that."

"I'm not really interested."

"Suit yourself. I am in desperate need of a proper thumping tonight."

"So I see. What happened to Bryce?"

"Oh, Bryce is a dag. He's just not my type."

"What do you mean?"

"I don't know, he's too much of an open book. There's no mystery about him. I like men with a hint of danger. Bryce is studying to be a kindergarten teacher."

"But don't you want to marry a nice guy?"

"Marry? Why would I want to get married?"

"Are you kidding?"

Sydney turned to look at me and burst out laughing.

"Lindsay, don't look so aghast! You're too sweet. Not all of us want to get married and have babies."

"You mean, you really don't? You're happy by yourself?"

"Very."

"What happens when you get older?"

"I'm not worried about it. For now, I've got my health, my family, my friends, a beautiful house...what more could I ask for?"

"But don't you want someone to share your life with?"

"If I meet someone and he makes me happy, why not? But if it doesn't happen, I'm not going to be miserable about it. I can always find someone to meet my needs."

"Apparently."

"You worry too much Lindsay."

She turned to look at me suspiciously.

"Have you been reading *Cosmo* again?"

"Sydney, stop! It has nothing to do with *Cosmo*."

I watched as she raised a challenging eyebrow.

"OK, well, not entirely. I mean, don't you want to have kids?"

"I don't know. I could go either way really. If I get to forty and I still haven't had any, I might adopt a little girl from China."

"I can't believe you're so casual about everything."

"Lindsay, you worry far too much. You need to focus all that nervous energy on having some fun."

"Well, at least one of us doesn't have trouble in that department."

Chapter Four
March

The Kelly Family

This weekend Sydney took me to Pi Ha. It was incredible: a breathtakingly rugged beach, with black sand sparkling with iron. It was so beautiful and unspoiled, I felt as though I was on a remote corner of the earth, which I suppose I was.

Sydney's mother, Peach, had invited me to spend this Easter weekend with the family but rescinded on the offer after her daughter Jill had another falling out with her Australian boyfriend. Apparently, the Kelly's are going away to their beach house for some kind of family discussion. Peach is a former secretary, married to the partner of the oldest law firm in Wellington. She reminds me of a character from a soap opera, chain smoking Benson and Hedges, and having a glass of gin and tonic every night before dinner. Today's "crisis," she told us, was a dying rat on the lawn that required several phone calls to find a man to remove it. Peach gave me a ride home in her red BMW convertible, which her husband had insisted on buying her because every woman should have a "fun" car, didn't I agree?

Peach suggested that I spend Easter weekend with Drew's family in Hamilton because as a mum, she would worry if she thought I was in Onetai, alone. I doubted the wisdom of this suggestion, mainly because I would feel like a girlfriend, who isn't a girlfriend. I had a long talk with Drew and explained my misgivings about spending a family holiday together. He insisted there was nothing to worry about. I wasn't convinced.

Affirmations
This is the best year of my life
I am comfortably and easily adapting to life in New Zealand
I am a brave, confident, capable woman

Love, Possibly?
Sydney thinks I'm in serious denial about my feelings for Drew. I keep telling her that we're just friends but she isn't convinced.

"Are you sure you don't fancy him even a teensy bit?" she asked me yesterday. We were sitting outside on her pool deck, working on an international languages assignment that I was redoing for the fifth time.

"He's not even divorced yet."

"I think he's really sweet."

"Well, his ex-wife keeps leaving messages on the answering machine saying that she'd like to throttle me."

"There's a surprise."

"And then she comes over and sits at the kitchen table as though nothing has happened. I think she's trying to intimidate Drew into signing an unfavorable custody agreement."

"Poor thing. He seems like such a sweet guy."

"So how are things with your guy?"

"Let's change the subject, shall we?"

No Sleep 'til Hamilton
Dear Diary,
I'm beginning to have second thoughts about motherhood.

On Friday night, Drew and I made the six hour trip to Hamilton. I never knew that life with a three year old could be so exhausting. We tried to be careful not to pass any golden arches, because once Miles sees McDonald's, whatever plans we have immediately get changed. Despite our best efforts, we still ended up driving towards one of the restaurants with the infamous yellow logo—and not just any restaurant. This one had a Play Land as well. As soon as Miles saw it, the pleading began.

"I want a Happy Meal, Daddy. Daaa—aad. I want a Happy Meal."

"Maybe later Miles."

Whenever Miles asks for something and Drew wants to say "no" he says "maybe later," instead. Miles has started to catch on to this, so he's no longer so easily fooled.

"Daddy! Daddy! I want a Happy Meal! I want a Happy Meal! Daaaa-aaaad!"

Miles kept repeating that he wanted a Happy Meal what seemed like at least eighty-seven times while Drew kept saying "maybe later". Then the tears came, which aren't as bad as the loud shrieks. Drew says that Miles is having some kind of delayed terrible twos behavior. I wanted to tell him that personally, I think he's become spoiled from being bought so many presents from both sides of his warring families, but I bit my tongue.

We took Miles to McDonald's for dinner so that he could play in the children's area and burn off some energy. Drew preferred to sit near the slides where there were other families with children whining, crying and spilling Coke on the floor. I make a mental note to myself not to say "other" families again.

I find that a lot of people look at us with curiosity, which is not surprising. Drew and I look like a young married couple in our late twenties, except that neither of us wears a ring. Miles definitely looks like Drew's son, with his chestnut hair and green eyes. And then of course, there's my "American accent". It feels strange to be told that I have a "lovely accent" but I take it as a compliment (like the word "bula" which, it turns out, isn't a compliment or an insult. It's Fiji for "hi").

After Miles finished playing with his food, spilled ketchup down his T-shirt and had a fight over a plastic toy with a fierce looking five-year-old girl, we finally left. Drew stopped for drinks at a local dairy and introduced me to the energy drink, "Vector". He warned me not to give any to Miles, who of course, immediately wanted some. This began a new chorus of pleading that lasted another fifteen minutes, making me wish I had accepted Bryce's invitation to a cricket match on the island where he lives. Or that I had just stayed home.

***

The next three hours felt like an eternity. Drew played songs and stories on the cassette deck to amuse Miles, but the imperious toddler doesn't seem to appreciate the effort. We had to stop more than once for Drew to change Miles' "nappies" which Drew told me I'm welcome to pitch in and help with anytime. I declined this dubious privilege, and silently cursed myself for forgetting my extra-strength Tylenol at home. I had a Titanic headache from listening to the same children's songs, over and over again. Miles especially likes "Five Little Ducks" which must be the most annoying children's song ever invented:

> *Five little ducks went out one day, over the hills and far away*
> *Mother duck said, quack, quack, quack, quack*
> *But only four little ducks came back*
> *Four little ducks went out one day...*

When we finally arrived at Helena's house it was midnight, and Miles was thankfully sound asleep, clutching his Paddington Bear. Drew's grandmother, Yolanda, was also there and I began to feel awkward, realizing that they'd want to speak to Drew alone about Janine.

We sat in the living room, which was filled with Royal Dalton figurines and Wedgwood, while Yolanda and Helena made small talk. I couldn't stop yawning, and finally excused myself to go to sleep. I can't say that Helena was very warm or friendly towards me, but I guess she has her reasons.

"Calimera" and Other Greek Delicacies

"'Kalimera'! Can you say 'Kalimera' Miles?"

Yolanda is trying to teach Miles to say "good morning" in Greek. Unfortunately, Miles does not seem to care for learning Greek, nor for Yolanda, a tall stocky woman with steel grey hair and pale blue eyes, who always seems to be finding a new fault, whether real or imagined, with her great-grandson.

Helena's garden outside is beautiful, and I decided to take a few pictures with Miles. Then, Drew, Miles and I went for a walk to a Chinese garden. It felt like spring, although I guess it's fall since the seasons are reversed.

Miles and I played together while Drew went to buy ice-cream. He loves the swings, and I pushed him while a couple of children stopped to watch.

"Is that your little boy?"

I looked down and a pig-tailed girl with freckles was squinting up at me. She couldn't be more than six years old. Miles was also looking at me, as though curious to hear my response.

"Well, he's…" My voice trailed off as I thought about what to say.

"Well, he's a special boy in my life."

Both the little girl and Miles seemed happy with this answer but I wasn't sure it was the right one.

Ladies Who Lunch

I've noticed that some women are absolutely fanatical about eating outside. I can't understand why. It seems like such a production to me, carrying cutlery and plates all the way from the kitchen, out to the lawn. The wind is usually blowing and napkins are lost, there's always a fly drowning in my beverage, and no matter how much sunscreen I wear, I end up with a burnt nose.

Today was no exception. Helena and Yolanda were bound and determined that we would all eat outside, even though Drew complained bitterly. It took almost half an hour to get the chairs properly set up, and move everything we needed from the kitchen out to the lawn. Helena poured me a large glass of juice, and two minutes later there was a green bottle fly swimming inside that made my stomach turn. I could feel the sun beating down on my face and arms, and was sure that I was developing melanoma.

"He's not eating his meat, Drew!" Yolanda peered at Miles disapprovingly.

I could see that this was not going to go well. Drew had already confessed to me that he thinks Miles' eating habits have been influenced by one of Janine's friends, a vegetarian prostitute. I have no idea how Janine even manages to make friends, but the company she keeps is definitely interesting, to say the least.

My sunglasses kept slipping off my nose, as I tried to watch my manners, knowing that Yolanda is a very proper Kiwi lady who used to write an etiquette column for the newspaper. Drew tells me that she and Helena have had high tea in Singapore. I'm impressed.

Helena and Yolanda remind me of the South Pacific version of the "Ladies Who Lunch" that Brian (my Toronto hair stylist) tends to cater to. "The Ladies Who Lunch" are Toronto's women of leisure, who come to have their hair done while shopping with their husbands' credit cards. I personally would have no objection to being a Lunch Lady. Instead, I'm the Poor Lady, gazing wistfully at the new spring and summer collections in Holt Renfrew by designers that I can't afford. I can't even afford Brian, but somehow I manage.

Although Helena is no longer married, she is definitely a Lunch Lady, and one who shops in Singapore where she has her clothes custom made (when she's not having high tea, I suppose). She tells me that she's going on a much-needed vacation to the Gold Coast. *A vacation from what?* I wonder. *The woman doesn't work.*

"Drew, what's the matter with the boy? Doesn't he eat at home?"

I'm jarred out of my musings by Yolanda, who is still harping about Miles' fussy eating habits.

Drew is beginning to look agitated, so I reach over and put Miles on my lap.

"Here, sweetheart. Shall we just have a little bit?"

I cut Miles' meat into bite-size pieces, and he happily lets me feed him. (This is a trick that my mother used with me.)

"Helena! The girl has him on her lap! Are you alright Lindsay?"

"She's fine mother! Do shut up."

"There aren't too many girls like you Lindsay," Helena says, finally beginning to warm up to me.

Er…probably not, I think to myself. I do want Helena to like me, but on the other hand, I hope she doesn't like me too much.

"Drew's got baggage you know," she later tells me privately in the kitchen, as I help her wash the dishes. I'm not too sure how to take this comment. Is it a warning before getting involved with him? And how does she know I want to get involved with him when I'm not even sure I want to get involved with him? Or maybe she's being hopefully optimistic that our friendship will grow into romance as we spend time together, when I would be the logical choice as the next Mrs. Andrew Theodore Christianson.

"Well, I think Miles is so much fun. He's adorable. I don't think anyone would look at Drew as having baggage. I actually think he's got a lot to offer."

Helena looks at me thoughtfully and says again, "There aren't many girls like you, Lindsay."

I realize that I have said too much, too soon, but it's too late.

Later that afternoon when I catch my reflection in the mirror, I see that my nose is sunburned. I guess some things in life are inevitable.

Cruise Ships and Canadiana

"Where are you from in Canada, Lindsay?"

"Mississauga. It's a suburb just outside Toronto."

Yolanda has taken a special interest in me. She has fond memories of Canada, which she visited often in her youth. Helena has also been and the two women reminisce about the maple leaves they remember seeing while taking a train across the country.

"Yes, maple syrup. You have that on your pancakes, don't you?"

"Yes."

"And salmon. You eat so much salmon!"

"Umm..." I don't think we eat that much salmon, but by now I've been away from my homeland so long that my mind starts playing tricks on me. I try to take an educated guess at what she might be talking about.

"Maybe in the Atlantic provinces. I guess people eat a lot of fish and seafood there."

Yolanda is no longer listening.

"When I used to take the cruise ship over, it was salmon for breakfast, salmon for tea, and salmon for supper!"

She is very indignant, and appears to be asking for an explanation from me.

"Well, it's funny that they served..."

Yolanda is impassioned now and cuts me off.

"I was just sick of it! Sick of it! It's all you Canadians eat! Salmon! Salmon! Salmon!"

I look at Helena who bursts into laughter. Drew joins in and I try to keep a straight face, then start laughing as well. Miles is gleefully playing with his food and bangs his fork on his plate.

"What's so funny? Helena? Why is everybody laughing?"

"Never mind, Mother. Never mind."

"Lindsay, you must come and visit me in Brisbane. I have a house there."

"That sounds nice, Yolanda."

"Yes, you must come and visit. Now, the boy isn't eating his meat again. What's the matter with him, Drew?"

We all turn to look at Miles who promptly spits his food out of his mouth and into his plate.

"Those manners! Shocking. Drew, is this what you teach him at home?"

Drew glowers at her.

"He ate well at lunch with Lindsay," Helena says.

"Lindsay! Lindsay! Lindsay!" Miles bangs his fork on the table.

"I think he just likes saying your name."

A Family Affair

Later that evening, I was reading in my room when Helena knocked on the door. She looked very excited and I could see Yolanda standing behind her in the hallway.

"Lindsay, we have something for you."

I follow Helena to her bedroom and she says, "Now, I don't want you to feel like you have to say yes, but I was talking to my Mum and we both agreed that we want you to have this."

She opens a mahogany jewellery box on top of her dresser, takes out a red cardboard box, and hands it to me. I open it and there's a blue glass cameo necklace inside.

"It's a family heirloom, it belonged to my grandmother."

"Helena, I can't accept something like that."

"No, we want you to have it," says Yolanda.

"Only if you'll wear it," says Helena.

"Yes, only if you'll wear it."

"Of course I'll wear it," I say. "It's beautiful."

Yolanda then gives Drew fifty dollars for the two of us to go to the movies. *Wow*, I think to myself, *they must really want him to get remarried...*

I wondered whether to say anything to Drew about his family's attempts at playing matchmaker, and decided against it. Then changed my mind.

"So, that was quite a compliment this evening."

"They really like you Lindsay." He looks happy.

We drove to the movie theatre where I suggested we see *Along Came Polly*, a comedy with Ben Stiller and Jennifer Aniston. Ten minutes into the movie, I realized that it might not have been the best choice. Ben Stiller's character discovers that his wife is cheating on him and the divorce proceedings send him into a downward spiral of depression. I look over at Drew and he's nodding his head as though agreeing with the fickleness of women.

But then Ben meets Jennifer, a carefree Bohemian spirit who infuses his life with laughter. "Polly" takes him salsa dancing and introduces him to a life free of the constraints imposed upon him by his uptight wife…"Lisa". At the end of the movie, Ben must make the choice between his cheating, superficial wife, who has the support of his parents, and his newfound love "Polly". I don't know which woman to root for and feel utterly confused.

When the movie is over, Drew says something to the effect that it was good, and he was thinking of his own personal situation as he watched it.

"I was thinking, yes, I should just go for Polly—I mean Lindsay— uh—Lisa—I mean—not the wife. You know what I mean."

I have no idea what he means, and decide not to ask for further explanation. Drew decides he wants to take me to the local Irish pub for a drink, and we walk over together. Sitting down across from him, I felt as though I was seeing him as a guy for the first time, as opposed to a hen-pecked ex-husband and son.

He was wearing a black turtleneck sweater and as he drank his beer, I realized how *hot* he was, taking in his clean-cut good looks, and muscular build. His Mum had given him money to get his hair cut and I was impressed at the result. He looked *really good*. I was also completely charmed by his accent.

It was exciting. I was out for the night with a real Kiwi, having a beer at an Irish pub, and listening to U2, Saturday night on Easter weekend in New Zealand. Drew seemed relaxed for the first time since I had met him. We talked a bit about our high school years and stayed out until 2 am.

And as we pulled up in the gravel driveway in front of his mother's house, I wondered whether Sydney was right. Maybe I did "fancy" him, just a bit.

A Perfectly Lovely Afternoon

"Will you come and play with us, Auntie Lindsay?"

Drew's seven-year-old niece was standing in the doorway holding a doll and looking up at me. I felt a slight shock, realizing that no one had ever called me "Auntie" before. I felt like I was taking an accelerated course: The Christianson Family 101. Drew's brother, his wife and their kids were over for Easter dinner. I was helping Helena chop vegetables in the kitchen when she introduced me to her son, Owen.

"This is Drew's flatmate, Lindsay," she announced, beaming.

"We call her 'Lovely Lindsay.'"

"Easy Mum," said Owen, grabbing a beer from the fridge. I had no idea what to say and nearly chopped off one of my fingers.

The evening meal was a typical Christianson family affair. Yolanda complained about Miles' table manners while Helena kept telling her to "shut up". Everyone ate too much, and the kids dragged me off to play with them in the garden. The other adults had their tea and discussed the trust account they're establishing for Miles that will keep The Best Thing That Ever Happened blocked from the family fortune.

As far as Easter weekends on the other side of the world go, I could have done worse, I suppose.

Tonight's Affirmations

This is the best year of my life

Every day, in every way,

My life in New Zealand gets better and better

I wait in serene stillness, knowing my husband is on the way

Chapter Five
April

An Authentically Relaxing Weekend
   Dear Diary,
   Last week, when Friday arrived, I fled to The Hyatt Regency, knowing full well I couldn't afford it. On the other hand, I didn't think I could afford to catch pneumonia or have a complete physical meltdown from inhaling all of the toxic pollen that has slowly been invading my body. I told myself that I would find a job with a law firm during my first school holiday and recuperate my financial losses.
   I chose a hotel that has the first full service spa in New Zealand and arrived wearing my Juicy Couture T-shirt. The concierge up-graded my room from a standard, to a junior suite with a view of the harbor. Yes!
   I was supposed to be organizing my life and catching up on my assignments, but between the spa, the satellite TV, free newspapers, magazines, and the fitness center, I was in no mood to study. I had the most amazing "stress release" massage on Friday night, ordered room service for breakfast, lazed around in my bathrobe, watched the ships in

the harbour, went back to sleep in my fluffy bed and later explored the city. So much for my student budget. And my credit card.

At least I got to be a tourist in Wellington, if only for a weekend. I also had a good talk with "Doris," the masseuse from the spa. She was very friendly and told me that she knows all the "cool places" to go to in Wellington on the weekend. I'm not sure whether to take her up on her offer to go out because I think she might be a lesbian. Or a high-paid prostitute. Or both. I have no idea. I have no "gaydar". She definitely looks like a tomboy, skinny and flat-chested, with very short blonde hair and blue toe nails.

Doris told me that New Zealand is nearly fifty years behind Hungary, where she is from. I'm not exactly sure what she meant by this (fifty years behind socially? politically?) but I said, "Yeah, I know what you mean!" anyway. She's planning to go home soon, but promised me some free passes to the health club before she leaves.

I might call her. Then again, maybe I won't.

Trouble in Paradise

Last night, Drew and I went to see *Spider Man 2* at the Paradise movie theatre. We had ordered our tickets online, but when we got to the theatre, the computer that processes online reservations was down. Other moviegoers were arriving and purchasing tickets with cash, then going ahead to get their seats in the theatre.

I started fretting there wouldn't be any good seats left, and went over to the usher to see if there was anything he could do.

"Excuse me," I said politely. "The computer that processes online ticket reservations is down, and I was wondering whether you could let us through with our receipts or call someone, maybe a manager, to help?"

He looked completely stunned by this request.

"Having a bad night are we?" asked someone sarcastically, behind me.

Now it was my turn to be confused. Drew later told me that Kiwis never complain about anything. It's part of their culture to shut up and "have a grumble" later on at home.

"I don't understand," I said.

"The whole point of paying more to reserve ahead of time is to make sure that you get a good seat. Those other people didn't reserve and they were being let in ahead of us. Don't you see something wrong with that?"

Drew didn't.

"So, if you ordered a bowl of soup and it was cold, you wouldn't send it back?"

"No."

"So you'd eat cold soup and then go home and complain about it? What's the point? Oh…forget it. I'll never understand this culture."

Tonight's Affirmations
I am a patient and culturally sensitive person
I am comfortably and easily adapting to life in New Zealand
I am willing to see things differently,
No matter how weird they may seem

The Proverbial Morning After
Or,
Sex Happens
Dear Diary,

Some women, like Sydney, are able to have sex with a million different men without ever developing feelings for them. I am not one of those women. Last night, I finally succumbed to Drew's charms after drinking one too many orange cream vodka coolers. I shouldn't blame the alcohol though, because it wasn't nearly as responsible for my lapse in judgment as Drew's new cologne, and the *Jerry McGuire* video we rented to watch together.

I was having breakfast with Drew and Bryce this morning, when I committed my first faux pas after having casual sex: Acting as though I just had meaningful sex. We were all having a friendly debate at the table about Drew's latest research paper, examining whether single women or single men make more purchases for their pets. I wasn't convinced of the merit of Drew's research, and was tempted to ask how exactly it relates to psychiatric nursing, but decided to choose my academic battles.

"Men make more money, so they spend more," I said.

"Women are the ones who make more actual purchases," argued Drew, who was passionately debating the topic in between large bites of peanut butter on toast. He looked even sexier than usual, freshly shaven and wearing a new navy turtleneck sweater. Without thinking, I leaned over to brush a crumb from his cheek.

"I think you missed a spot," said Bryce, dryly.

I felt my cheeks grow warm, but before I could think of something witty to say in response, the phone rang. Drew grabbed the cordless receiver and I could tell from his tone of voice that it was Janine on the other end of the line.

"Hello? Hiya. Just getting ready to go to school...Yup, yup. I'll come 'round this afternoon after I finish up at the college..."

I tried to keep my facial expression neutral but of course, nothing escapes Bryce and he looked at me pointedly, raised an eyebrow, then smirked and left the table.

There was a sinking feeling in the pit of my stomach as I wondered why Drew was going over to Janine's house. Had she blown an electrical fuse again? Was Miles sick? I told myself that absolutely nothing had changed since yesterday—Drew was still my flat mate, and we were still technically not an item. Having sex and having a relationship are two different things. Or so I tried to convince myself.

After what seemed like an eternity of listening to Drew say, "Yup, yup," he finally said goodbye and hung up the phone.

I had promised myself to count to ten before asking what Janine wanted, but just like one of my ambitious New Year's Resolutions, it was impossible to keep.

"Was that Janine?"

"Yup."

"How's she doing?"

"Good."

"Anything new?"

"Not really."

"Then...why are you going over to her house?"

"Sweets, I'm just going with her to talk to Miles' teacher. He's been acting up a bit at school, and they want both parents to come in."

"Oh."

Right. Parents. I wasn't one of those, although technically, all of my efforts should really count for something.

"Sweets, why don't we go for a nice dinner tonight? I've been wanting to take you to my favourite restaurant." Drew was putting his breakfast dishes away, and I half-wondered whether to join him in the car so we could talk a bit longer, but I'd promised Bryce to help him with some research at the library this morning.

"Sure, sounds good," I said, doubtfully.

He leaned over to kiss the top of my head, and I watched as he pulled on his rain jacket, slung his knapsack over his shoulder and headed towards the door, leaving a lingering trail of cologne behind him.

"Have a good day, Sweets."

"Bye."

I felt my throat constrict. What has gotten into me? I've never felt jealous of Janine before.

***

"Didn't your mother ever teach you about oxytocin?" asked Sydney, when I told her my story four hours later. We were sitting in the cafeteria, sharing a ham and cheese pie while Sydney worked on our latest international languages assignment. The cafeteria was overcrowded as usual, and I had a hard time hearing her above the raucous laughter coming from the table beside us. A group of physical education students were taking turns throwing popcorn in the air and catching it in their mouths.

"Oxy—*what*? What are you talking about?"

"Oh Lindsay. Oh dear." She started laughing as though I had just told her the most hysterical joke in the world.

"Sydney! This isn't funny. What are you laughing about?'

"Lindsay, you're feeling attached to Drew because you just had sex with him."

"What do you mean, 'attached to him'? I'm not attached to him."

"Oh, really? When was the last time you brushed a crumb of toast off his cheek?"

A fresh peal of laughter rang out from a group of girls sitting on our other side. I was starting to feel like the entire universe was enjoying an inside joke at my expense.

"That's beside the point. I promised myself not to get involved with Drew because he's still—I mean, technically..." I was at a loss for words.

"Go on." Sydney looked as though she was enjoying herself a smidge too much.

"Well, technically, I mean legally, he's separated. His divorce isn't final for another three months, so I don't want to 'date' him yet."

"Right. Then what do you call dinner at the restaurant tonight?"

"What do you mean? I eat dinner with him every night—we're flat mates."

"With benefits."

"Very funny."

"You know Lindsay, there are times when sex can lead to dating."

"This is not one of those times. I made a personal resolution not to date Drew until his divorce is final."

"Oooh...deadly. Didn't you tell me you always end up breaking your resolutions?" Sydney asked with a wicked smile on her face. Damn. I confide far too much in that woman. I wondered whether she'd been spending time with Bryce again, but decided not to ask.

"Tell me what this oxy-thing is."

"Oxytocin. It's a bonding chemical that's released after a woman has sex. It's what makes you fall in love with a bloke. Nature's way of ensuring babies. Haven't you ever wondered what makes you want to cuddle after sex?"

"Not really. I just thought it was normal."

"It is normal. What's happening to you right now is normal. You just have to recognize it for what it is, and not get caught up in the emotion."

"So, are you saying everything I'm feeling is caused by chemicals?"

"Pretty much. Try doing a Google search for oxytocin. Now—let's finish this assignment, shall we?"

***

As soon as I got home from school, I ran up the stairs to Drew's computer and typed "oxytocin" into the Google browser. The first 'hit' said: *Oxytocin: The Hormone of Love.* According to the resident expert at teenwire.com:

> *Oxytocin is a hormone that is produced in the body. It is released during the arousal, excitement, and orgasm stages of the sexual response cycle. It is also released through non-sexual physical contact, such as cuddling. It can cause feelings of warmth and relaxation and a decrease in stress. It is believed that oxytocin is associated with emotional connections and feelings of love.*

Wonderful. Apparently, I'm not just playing with fire, I'm tempting my whole chemical circuitry to fall in love with a practically-married man. This does not bode well for several reasons:

a) My mother would kill me if she knew.
b) So would my father.
c) So would Drew's mother. And grandmother.

But the important thing is, they would be happy to know we're not actually dating. On the other hand, I can't say that anyone would be in a rush to send their congratulations about the wanton sex that we just had. I still don't think sleeping together, under the circumstances, is as bad as dating, but maybe I'm just deluded. Or falling in love. Or both. I blame the oxytocin. They should call it *oxytoxin*—apparently it destroys whatever's left of your capacity for rational thought.

Affirmations
This is the best year of my life
I am not attached to Drew
I am the opposite of attached
I am a brave, confident, capable woman

Extreme Make-Under
This afternoon, I forced Drew to give me his honest opinion on everything in my closet.

"What do you think of this skirt? Is it too *flash*?"

"What do you mean *flash*? You've been saying that a lot lately. Anyway, it's fine, Lindsay. Your clothes are fine."

"What about this Juicy Couture T-shirt? Do you think it's too *flash* for teacher's college?"

"Dah'lin,' you look gorgeous in everything. You could wear a potato sack and still be a stunner."

"Then why does Jordy keep making fun of me? No matter what I wear, he's like, *Nice outfit*."

"Do you reckon he's taking the piss? I reckon he likes you."

"Jordy? No. Anyway Drew, please give me your honest, honest opinion."

"Ok, my honest, honest opinion is that you should come over here so I can kiss you."

"Drew! Be serious. OK, why don't you tell me which clothes make me stand out so I can put them away?"

"I reckon you're worrying too much Lindsay. Ok, Sweets, I have to get ready for work now."

"What? Are you on night shift?"

"Yup. Why don't you ask Bryce for his opinion?"

"Bryce? Oh yeah, why don't I just skewer myself and save him the trouble?"

"You're so cheeky."

"I know. That's why you like me."

I ended up going through the closet myself and put aside anything that remotely looked like it could be worn by Paris Hilton. I figured I was safe with plain T-shirts (no logos) and long jeans. I put away my dangling earrings and threw out all of my make-up except for the Bobbi Brown under-eye concealer. That should do it.

A Dining Disaster

Tonight, as it turns out, was my first unofficial date with Drew. When he picked me up from class, he had half a dozen red roses for me that made me sneeze as soon as I took them from him. These allergies are going to be the death of me.

Drew has been talking for over a week about taking me out to his favorite restaurant, but wouldn't tell me which one it was because he wanted it to be a surprise. When we pulled up in front of the restaurant, my heart sank. It was an East Indian restaurant and I've never been able to stomach curry. I told myself that it was a matter of making a mental attitude adjustment, but no amount of positive affirmations,

I am open to new culinary experiences,

I am an open-minded and adventurous eater,

would make the queasiness in my stomach go away.

The interior of the restaurant was a rich burgundy and the heaviness of the atmosphere somehow made me feel even more nauseous. When the server brought out our curry and nan bread, I was too focused on trying to get through the meal to register what Drew was saying to me.

"something, something, don't you agree?"

"I'm sorry?"

"Lindsay, you've hardly touched your food. Is everything all right?"

"Of course! It's delicious," I said, taking a bite of curry and trying not to gag as I swallowed. I felt my stomach heave. *Oh God.*

"I've noticed you don't eat very much. Are you anorexic?"

At that moment, I swallowed a large chunk of chicken that caught in my throat. I stared at Drew, gasping for breath and tried to signal to him that I was choking.

"...because it's nothing to be ashamed of. I'm a nurse, I understand these things. I know a good counselor who can help you work through your issues. Sweets? Are you alright?"

By now I had both hands to my throat, and was gasping for air and praying to God that Drew would STOP TALKING and do something before I choked to death. I had visions of ending up like Shelley Long in *Hello Again*. I was going to die choking on a piece of chicken and come back to my life as a ghost a year later, only to discover that everyone had moved on without me. Drew would be married to Sydney, who would be wearing the blue glass cameo necklace that Helena gave me. Damn Sydney. She's always said she thinks that Drew is "really sweet".

"Sweets, are you choking?"

Drew had finally clued in to the obvious.

I nodded my head, trying not to panic.

"SHE'S CHOKING! MY GIRLFRIEND'S CHOKING!"

A murmur of excitement went through the restaurant and the headwaiter ran over to our table.

Grabbing me from behind while Drew stared in horror, he put his arms around me to administer the Heimlich manoeuvre. The piece of chicken that was caught in my throat flew out of my mouth and hit Drew in the left eye.

"Ow! Bloody hell!"

"Sorry!" I gasped, trying to catch my breath.

I could feel the stares of everyone in the restaurant, and half-expected someone to say, *Having a bad night are we?*

"Why didn't you just tell me that you don't like Indian food?" Drew asked when we got home.

"I don't know. Because you were so excited about taking me to your favorite restaurant. I didn't want to disappoint you. Why don't you know how to do the Heimlich manoeuvre? Don't they teach you that at nursing school?"

"I don't take first aid until next semester. Alright Sweets, why don't you go lie down and rest. I'll make us an omelette for dinner."

So that was the (un)Official First Date.

I thanked God for sparing my life and not allowing me to die unmarried, and on the other side of the world. Next time, I'll just order salad.

Tonight's Affirmations
This is the best year of my life
I have inner strength more powerful than any current challenges
I am a brave, confident, capable woman

Chapter Six
May

Hair Today, Gone Tomorrow

The Best Thing That Ever Happened has threatened to scalp me again. Under different circumstances I might have found it amusing for another woman to take such an interest in me. However, given that she sounds serious about inflicting bodily harm, and since I find myself on the other side of the world without any family or friends, I have to admit, it is a bit troubling. If she follows through on her promise to chop off all my hair, I will cry. I have already had one hair disaster at Jon-Jon's Hair Salon in Wellington.

Drew drove me to the salon on Saturday morning because I couldn't wait anymore. Every day had become a Bad Hair Day. The frazzled hair stylist who greeted me was a blonde woman in her mid-twenties who did not seem sympathetic to my concerns about achieving the right hair color. I told her I would rather she take her time doing my highlights and said I'd come back for a trim later when she was less busy. But no, she insisted on doing both in haphazard fashion, and was either deaf or deliberately chose to ruin my life. Instead of giving me touch-ups in the same shade of caramel that Brian put in, and a trim to get rid of my split ends, she made my hair a deep shade of burgundy and cut what looked like six inches of hair off, resulting in tight, cork-screw curls.

"There's nothing you can do! The damage is done! I can't even look! Just—pin it up for me! "

Jon-Jon, the owner, had a box of bobby pins and was trying to pin my hair up while asking how he could make amends. Unfortunately, I couldn't stay to have my hair fixed (and how could it be fixed anyway, short of hair extensions, which I can't afford) because Drew had come to pick me up and left the car running with Miles inside.

"Hi."

"Hi." I couldn't look at him.

"Your hair looks...good."

The way he paused before saying "good" with his inflection rising at the end, told me that it did *not* look good. At all.

"Oh...Don't cry, Sweets. It's not that bad. Shivers! She's a bit emotional," he explained to my stylist.

Jon-Jon later said that he had never encountered anyone like me. Clearly, he was not familiar with the Lunch Ladies of Toronto. Or the Ladies of the Civello salon uptown where I've seen more than one woman scream at her stylist, creating regular afternoon dramas. I thought my reaction paled in comparison and told him so. Jon-Jon thought this was hilarious, and invited me back to personally redo my hair.

I wonder whether I should be worried about Janine. She has more time on her hands now that her boyfriend has left her. Helena says that she has nothing better to do during the day than dream up ways to prevent Drew from being happy (and traumatize me, I might add). She thinks that girls like Janine shouldn't be allowed to benefit from their mother's allowance and sit at home all day. I personally wish she *would* spend more time at home so that I'm not constantly looking over my shoulder, wondering whether she's going to take a pair of scissors to my remaining curls. Anyway, I have to find out how soon I can get my hair color changed. I'm going to have to wear a baseball cap in the meantime.

Affirmations
I am satisfied and content with my hair

I am grateful to still have some
I accept how I look at this moment
(even though I've just had the worst haircut of my life...)

Mr. Maybe
Dear Nathan,

Guess what? I think I've met someone. Remember how you warned me not to get involved in the conflict between Drew and his ex-wife? I'm thinking about just getting involved with Drew.

I know what you're going to say, and no, I'm not sure this is a good idea. It's just that he has so much of everything I've ever wanted in a guy. He's cute and smart, he's considerate (well, most of the time. He still keeps leaving the toilet seat up). He's a really caring person. I can see why he's doing so well in his nursing program.

If you met someone who had all or most of the qualities that you've been looking for but they were not quite available, would you wait for that person to become available?

I think he's pretty serious about me. It's just weird to think he's still married to Janine. In New Zealand, there's a mandatory two-year separation period before a couple can get divorced. So, it's not like he's deliberately stalling on that front but still...

Anyway, sounds like you had an interesting date on Friday night. No, I can't say that I've ever been out with someone who claimed to be a cat in a previous life, but it's an interesting thought. Maybe she's been reading The Celestine Prophecy.

Run, Nathan, run!
Love,
Lindsay

Dear Lindsay,

Are you sure this is a good idea? I don't think you should settle for "almost available". Remember the last time you didn't listen to your gut instinct and that guy you were dating ended up preferring guys? I've always told you, you see what you want to see.

Make him sweat it out for a while, and whatever you do, don't antagonize the ex. I'd try to steer clear of her.

I think you're better off with someone else, but you never listen to me. Think of him as Mr. Maybe.

Nathan

Everybody Needs Good Neighbors

Today has not been good. I was immobilized from menstrual cramps and Bryce and I had another fight over the TV. He refused to let me watch the series finale of *Friends* because the All Blacks football game was on.

Tension with Bryce has been building for the past couple of weeks since he found out that Drew and I are now (un)officially an item. He doesn't offer to make me coffee anymore when he's getting himself a cup, and he even goes into the bathroom to lift the toilet seat up after I've used it. Hmmm...and he wonders why I chose Drew instead of him.

Bryce finally left to go out for the evening, undoubtedly for a beer and a shag, and I was trying to finish a homework assignment but couldn't concentrate because someone had been using a power saw for the past hour. I had a pounding headache and finally couldn't take it anymore. I threw on a sweater and went outside to see where the noise was coming from. I asked the next-door neighbors if they were using a power saw.

"No," said the couple on the other side of the gate. "It isn't us, it's the new family that just moved in on the other side."

"At eleven o'clock at night?" I asked, incredulously.

It was terrible, we all agreed.

"It's just so rude. It's disturbing the entire neighborhood. Aren't there any bylaws about noise?"

It turned out there were, but the couple was afraid to say anything because they had recently immigrated to the country and were intimidated by the Professor and his wife. I couldn't understand why they were living in Onetai, but didn't ask any more questions.

"Well, don't worry," I said. "I'll go over and speak to him."

I didn't end up speaking to the Professor, but to his wife, Pippa.

"Hi," I said, "I was just wondering how much longer your husband will be because it's kind of late, and the noise is disturbing the other neighbors."

"Oh?"

"Well, yes. I'm just letting you know that it's bothering a few people."

"My husband is a professor at the university."

"Right. I was just wondering whether it's going to be much longer."

"Edward teaches day and evening classes, and this is the only time he can work in the garage. I'm sure you understand, love. Where are you living, then?"

"Uh..."

"Edward! Edward, come here!"

Damn. I wanted to run back to the house but she'd probably tell the rest of the neighbors and I'd never live down the gossip.

"What is it?"

"This young lady—what did you say your name was?"

"It's Lindsay." I fidgeted nervously with my Ronald McDonald hair.

"Lindsay has just come over to let us know that the neighbors are disturbed by the power saw."

"Are you American?" He looked amused.

"Canadian."

"Canadian! My brother lives in Canada. How long have you been here?"

"A few months now."

"What brought you to New Zealand?"

"Teacher's college."

"Teacher's college! Is that right? Well, we'll have to have you 'round for tea, won't we Pippa? She can meet Chelsea and Luke."

"Yes. I'm sure Chelsea could use some help with her homework. It's going to be handy having a teacher next door. Lindsay, can I get you something fizzy to drink?"

"No thank you. I should probably get back to my assignment."

"Alright then, cheers!"

My heart sank as I walked back to the house and wondered what I had got myself into this time.

Damn.

Back to Jon-Jon's Hair Salon

Drew took me back to Jon-Jon's hair salon this weekend. I chatted with Jon-Jon while he did my hair and pointed to a model in *Australian Vogue.*

"I really like her style."

"I'll tell her you said so."

I looked at Jon-Jon and had no idea what to say. This is exactly the kind of comment Kiwis make that throw me off guard. Does he know the model or is he being sarcastic for no particular reason?

I mentioned that Dale, the drama coach at Tutage Teacher's College, told me that Peter Jackson is casting for *King Kong*. Jon-Jon said he wouldn't mind being in the movies and asked if I know how to go about getting an agent. It seems like every second person I meet here has acting ambitions, I assume because of the success of *The Lord of the Rings*. Even Drew has been making noises about wishing he could go on auditions with me, but he can't because he has to work and look after Miles for the next fifteen years.

"Yes, your life is over at thirty-two," I teased him.

"Don't worry, Drew. I'm sure one day you and Jon-Jon will make it big as extras. At least sometime before you turn fifty!"

Drew looked as though he didn't know whether to smile or scowl.

"You're so cheeky!"

Dinner For Three

I'm having trouble understanding the animosity towards Americans that is rampant on this island (or maybe just amongst the Kiwis that I end up staying with). George Bush seems to be a popular topic of conversation and dislike of Canada's neighbor to the south extends to popular culture as well as foreign policy.

My Kiwi neighbors invited me over for dinner and I didn't know how to say "no." I *knew* I shouldn't have complained about the power saw. The kids had eaten their meal earlier and were in the lounge watching *New Zealand Idol*. Our dinner conversation went something like this:

Edward:

"So what kind of television shows do you like to watch?"

Me:

"Oh, you know, just a few. *Friends*, *Will & Grace*..."

Pippa:

"Oh...*American* programs. We don't like those do we?"

Edward:

"No."

Pippa:

"We prefer British programs don't we?"

Edward:

"Yes."

Pippa:

"Yes."

Edward:

"We don't like those…what are they called? Sitcoms. American sitcoms with…what is it called? Canned laughter. They aren't funny."

Pippa:

"No, no. American television isn't funny. We don't like it, do we?"

Edward:

"No. We prefer British shows."

Me:

"Oh. What about *The Office*? That's British isn't it? I hear it got great reviews."

Pippa:

"We don't like *The Office* do we?"

Edward:

"No, no."

Pippa:

"No. Don't you like any other British programs?"

Me:

"Well, we don't get too many. Mostly American. I suppose everyone likes what they're brought up watching."

Pippa (Ignoring my attempt at diplomacy):

"Oh, and the American MOVIES. Terrible. And what's that show about the dysfunctional family—*Malcolm in the Middle*? Who would want to watch a show about a dysfunctional family?"

Clearly, Pippa was not familiar with the majority of popular American television. I felt very, very relieved that I had not mentioned my passion for *Sex and the City* because—aside from all the "dysfunction," there's a lot of sex that the Kiwi couple would probably not find funny in the least. I don't get the impression there's ever been any sex in this house since the birth of their last child.

Pippa:

"…Lindsay?"

Me:

"I'm sorry?"

I realized the topic of conversation had suddenly changed.

Pippa:

"I said, Chelsea won her netball match today!"

Me:

"That's great!"

Edward (self-importantly):

"Yes, netball is New Zealand's national sport for girls."

(Discussion about netball and Canadian women's hockey ensues)

Then, I foolishly, foolishly bring up the subject of a history book about New Zealand that traces socio/cultural/political origins of New Zealand's settlers. A discussion comparing the Puritan Settlers in North America and settlers in New Zealand is a total fiasco as Edward and Pippa, who have about nine degrees between them, cannot answer any of my questions and we all quickly realize how embarrassing this is to them.

Edward (smiling):

"Well. Australia was settled by convicts of course."

Me:

"Of course! My father warned me not to become an Aussie's 'Sheila.'"

Pippa:

"What happened?"

(I am momentarily silent while I try to figure out whether or not I should be insulted.)

Edward (Trying to salvage any semblance of decency as I continue to sit in shocked silence...or perhaps upon reflection, he was completely oblivious and trying to score an intellectual point...):

"'Sheila' is *Australian*." (Angrily)

Pippa:

"No, we say 'Sheila.'"

Edward:

"*No*, it's old!"

Pippa:

"*No*, we still say it!"

Me:

"Well! Thank you very much for dinner. It was lovely."

Edward and Pippa in unison:

"Have some more!"

I sit back down reluctantly.

Pippa (smacking her lips):

"Mmmm...fish cakes. They're so hot and lovely to have when it's cold outside."

Me:

"Mmm hmm..."

Pippa:

"They make you feel all nice and toasty (smacks her lips again) mmm...mmm...I think it's the coriander that makes them so...*hot*."

Edward (exasperated),

"Oh...you *do* go on!"

(Oh God, not more fighting)

Pippa glares at her husband and I say a silent prayer that they don't invite me over again. There's enough drama in my own house.

In the spirit of being a global ambassador for my country, I decided I'd try watching some British TV, although the actors tend to be about as attractive as Probable Lawyer/Not Good Looking At All. I wonder whether he ever made it on time for his wedding?

Tonight's Affirmations

I am an open-minded and culturally sensitive person

I am not a tall poppy

I am comfortably and easily adapting to life in New Zealand

Chapter Seven
June

The Opposite of Jealous

I don't think Drew realizes how good-looking he is. He told me that when he was a teenager, he used to be overweight with acne and Coke bottle glasses. But like the ugly duckling that turned into a swan, he started working out and lost the weight, his skin cleared up, and now he wears contact lenses. The man is gorgeous.

Whenever we go out, other women flirt with him shamelessly, which drives me crazy. Take tonight, for instance. We were at the check out counter at the grocery store, and the cashier was staring at Drew as though it was her first time seeing a member of the opposite sex. Drew was completely oblivious as he tried to find his Cash Flow card

"I like your jersey," said the cashier seductively, leaning forward so that Drew had a clear view of her ample cleavage, coyly displayed by a low-cut blouse.

"Cheers. I just got it, actually."

"Oh really? Where from?"

"There's a place in Dressmart. Forget the name. They've got heaps of designers."

"Well, it's quoite noice on you. Do you live nearby?" she asked suggestively, twirling a strand of her poodle-permed hair, and batting a set of mascara-caked eyelashes.

"Yup, yup. Top of the road."

"I just moved here from Auckland."

"Cool."

The cashier parted her glossy lips, opening her eyes wide as she gazed at Drew.

"I'm absolutely knackered right now," she said dramatically, pulling back her elbows and tilting her head to the side, in what was ostensibly a stretch, but really just gave her an excuse to thrust her chest out.

"I wouldn't mind having a pint when this shift is over. Do you have a business card?"

By this time, I was thinking, *Hello? Can anyone see me?*

"Ashleigh," I interjected (her name tag said "Ashleigh").

"I'm sorry to interrupt, but I really need to get my boyfriend home. He won't be getting much sleep tonight, if you know what I mean!"

I winked at her conspiratorially while she glared back at me, grabbed our bags, and led an astonished-looking Drew out the door.

"Lindsay! What's gotten into you?"

"What's gotten into me? What's gotten into you, Mr. Casanova!"

"Have you gone mad?"

"Yes, I am mad!"

"No...I mean, are you crazy?"

"Because I didn't hand you a pen and paper when another girl practically asked for your number in front of me? How can you be so rude?"

"I'm the one who's rude? You're the one who told her we're going home to have sex! Do you think she was chatting me up? I reckon she was just being friendly. She's new to town."

"Just being friendly? Please! You 'reckon' everyone's just being friendly!"

"I don't say anything when Bryce chats you up and it's right in my own house!"

"That's because you don't want him to leave! You'd rather have his rent money to buy all your Hugo Boss shirts!"

"Still. What was he saying to you the other night? He's looking for a nice girlfriend 'purely for the sake of marriage and children'?"

"You're the one who's always telling me to be nice to him!"

"OK, Sweets. We're even."

***

We're not even, and that wasn't the point. Dating Drew is obviously going to be more of a challenge than I expected.

Affirmations
I am a beautiful, confident, capable woman
I am not jealous
I am the opposite of jealous
I am a total catch
I am a confident woman who deserves a man who's a total catch

Where the Boyfriends Are
Dear Diary,

Nathan emailed me this evening to tell me that my ex-best friend is getting married to an ex. My ex-best friend is Trish, who I met on our university cheerleading team. We used to do everything together from homework assignments to getting our first bikini wax. Unfortunately, the bikini wax isn't my only painful memory with my former friend. Trish ended up stealing my boyfriend, Todd. Out of the blue one day, he asked whether I'd ever consider a threesome with her, and it turned out that she had suggested it to him over a "friendly" lunch. I should have called her bluff, but instead I hit the roof and we had a huge fight that ended with Trish and Todd riding off into the sunset together.

This memory brought back others, as I remembered my years of marathon dating before I met Ben and my months of wasting time with "Mr. Wrongs" afterwards. Each relationship ended for different reasons, but I'm convinced that if I can find a pattern, it might help me understand how not to make the same mistakes again. I think what I need to do is a thorough evaluation of my entire dating history.

Let's see...

1. Conroy: Deported back to Trinidad.
2. T-Jay: A practising Jain from India whose religion forbids violence of any kind, including negative thoughts about another person. He told me I was a stumbling block to his spiritual growth.

3. Damian: A restaurant owner I met in Madrid while studying Spanish. He asked me to stay so we could get married and have lots of babies, but I wasn't mastering the language very well. I was afraid that I'd spend the rest of my life only understanding 60 per cent of my conversations with other people.

5. Todd: Stolen by my ex-best friend, Trish.

6. Troy: A professional baseball player that I met at Easy and the Fifth downtown. After eight months, I found out that I wasn't the only girl who thought she had an "exclusive" relationship with him.

7. Peter: Preferred guys.

8. Ben: No explanation required.

9. Dean: Toronto entertainment lawyer and former Calvin Klein model. At first it was exciting going to all of the "it" places, but I started to develop a complex about dating someone who was a better dresser, and better looking than I am. We lasted about four months until I had a mishap at the salon where an aesthetician over plucked my eyebrows. Dean told me that I didn't meet his "standards" anymore. (And Jon-Jon wondered what the big deal about my hair was...)

10. Landon: High school teacher with a passion for chess and TV game shows. I'm not sure what attracted me to him, but after three weeks of watching *Jeopardy!* and planning dates around Internet chess matches, I decided to take my mother's advice and focus on finding someone with at least one other common interest.

11. Jim: A University of Toronto professor who thought he had a really, really good sense of humor, but he really, really didn't. One day, he phoned me at work pretending to be a client who wanted to sue me for malpractice. By the time I figured out it was a "practical joke" I had already phoned my insurance company and scared the hell out of the partners in the firm who kept saying, "This guy's a university professor?" after I explained the misunderstanding.

12. Avery: Federal politician and megalomaniac who is convinced he will become Prime Minister when the country is hit by a national crisis that only he can solve. Similarly deluded about his sexual prowess.

And there we have it. In the final analysis, it looks like my relationship failures can be attributed to one of two things: Either the guy I dated was an idiot, or...hmm. Did I say two things?

They should really teach people how to develop good relationships, starting in high school. They could have mini-courses like communication with the opposite sex so that you can learn what a guy really wants (or doesn't want) when he says (or doesn't say) something, and remedial classes for when things start to get rocky. In fact, they should have relationship tutors. That's what I need.

So, Todd and Trish are finally getting married. Hmmm. Well, it's not a big deal. I'm having a year of adventure and wild romance in New Zealand. I'm fine.

9:00 pm

Who am I trying to kid? My life is a catastrophe.

9:15 pm

My life is a catastrophe with a capital "C." I'm turning thirty, and I'm having a pre-thirty meltdown, hoping that my Kiwi boyfriend will actually get the divorce that he's been promising. I've become one of those sorry women that you read about in the advice columns:

Dear E. Jean,

I love my boyfriend and he's everything I've ever wanted. The only problem is, he's still married. He promises that he's going to get a divorce as soon as...

And what do I think when I read those letters?

You're an idiot! Leave! Don't waste any more of your precious time with the wanker! Run, girl, run!

And so what do I do? I come all the way to New Zealand where there are more single men than I've ever seen in one building at Tutage Teacher's College and I don't go out with any of them. Instead, I get involved with my married landlord. Perfect.

9:45 pm

Why does it bother me so much that Todd and Trish are getting married? She's a traitor and he's a...well, he's a traitor too. They deserve each other.

10:00 pm

I miss Drew. I hate when he works at night. If he were here right now, he would know exactly what to say to make me feel better.

10:15 pm

I can't sleep. I'm too cold, and I keep thinking about how much I want to go to Trish and Todd's wedding so I can be the person who stands up and speaks now, instead of forever holding her peace. Damn Nathan. Why did he have to email and tell me?

10:30 pm

Damn Bryce. I just fell into the toilet again. I am never going to get used to living with these men.

12:30 am

I wonder if I'll ever get married, or if I'll just end up living with Drew in New Zealand for the next ten years, taking care of Miles and dodging phone calls from Janine. At least Drew doesn't seem to have any major character flaws, unlike most of the other men I've dated. The worst thing I've seen is a tendency to avoid responsibility, which I can probably live with. I like to think I've had an advantage by living with Drew before we started dating, since I've been able to really get to know him.

Affirmations

I am a smart, confident, capable woman

I am not jealous of Trish and Todd

I am the opposite of jealous

Too Much of a Good Thing

This weekend, Drew and I took the train from Wellington to Auckland, to do some sight-seeing and have dinner at the Auckland Sky Tower. The view was amazing, and we had a good walk around the observation deck, looking at the different parts of the city. The restaurant had a revolving floor, like the restaurant at the CN Tower in Toronto. Drew ordered lamb for dinner, with a bottle of New Zealand red wine, and then we went to the casino where I discovered his addiction to gambling.

Drew sat down at a slot machine called "Gypsy Rose" after paying $50.00 for a bucket of quarters. There was an older man sitting at a slot machine next to us dressed like Elvis, who kept saying, "Uh- huh-huh" every time he pulled the lever. Drew didn't even notice. He was staring intently at the buttons in front of him, muttering to himself as he dropped quarter after quarter into the slot machine.

He won $10, lost $5, won $100, then lost all of it.

"Cheap thrills," he said, shrugging his shoulders after the last token had disappeared.

"Do you have some kind of gambling addiction? We've been here for *four hours!*"

Bored, I had left him beside Elvis while I went to wander around the gift shop. I bought myself an over-priced copy of *The History of New Zealand*, and spent half an hour talking to a tourist from France who told me she had promised herself to visit New Zealand before she turns seventy next year. I felt at least seventy myself by the time Drew was ready to leave.

"Too much of a good thing can be a bad thing, you know."

"What's that, Sweets?"

Sigh.

"Never mind."

The Feijoa Doesn't Fall Far From the Tree
Or,
Forbidden Fruit

Last night, I had a strange dream. It was a sunny afternoon, and Drew had decided to take Miles and me to pick feijoas. We had to pry Miles away from the TV, which was no small task because, like his father, once he gets involved in an activity, it's hard to shift his focus to something else. Drew finally bribed him with a cookie, and I sat in the back of the car reading *Peter Pan* to him. We pulled up by the side of the gravel road where there was a field with a large feijoa tree, and a farmhouse in the distance.

"Are you sure we're allowed to pick fruit from this tree? Won't the owners mind?"

"No, don't worry Sweets. I know the people who own this property. It's alright."

Drew climbed the feijoa tree while Miles played with his Paddington Bear on the grass. I stood on the ground as Drew tossed feijoas to me, which I dropped inside a small cloth sack. A red pick up truck passed by, and two swarthy-looking men stared out at us from the cab. The driver looked like Bryce, except that he had a thick, curly moustache.

"Drew, I don't think this is such a hot idea."

Drew turned to look at the truck, but not before he absentmindedly tossed a feijoa in the air that landed on Miles' head.

"AAAAAAAAH!"

Miles wailed while I ran to pick him up and bounced him up and down on my hip.

"Miles, Miles. You're alright. You're OK. There's a good boy. Shall we go to McDonald's and get you a treat? Would that make it better?"

Miles perked up at the word "McDonald's" and the sobbing quickly subsided.

"Shall we go get some ice-cream with Daddy?" he asked hopefully.

"Daddy, shall we go get some ice-cream?"

"OK."

Drew climbed down from the tree as the two swarthy men got out of their truck and approached us.

"G'day," said Drew looking nervous.

"What you got there mate?" asked the heavier-set man who had a thick black moustache and bulging biceps.

"Just picked a few feijoas. We're off now."

"You're off, eh? Give us those."

Both Miles and I stared at Drew, waiting to hear what he'd say.

Before anyone could speak, a loud shot came from the farmhouse.

"Jesus! What was that?" asked the man who looked like Bryce.

Both men got back into the truck and sped off towards the farmhouse leaving behind a thick cloud of dust.

"I reckon we'll be on our way then," said Drew, picking up the sack of feijoas, as though nothing had happened.

"I want an ice cream Daddy! Daaa-aad! I want an ice-cream!"

***

I woke to the sound of Miles wailing in the kitchen downstairs.

"Daa-aady! I want some ice-cream!"

"Not for breakfast, Miles! Maybe later."

I could hear Drew opening and closing the kitchen cupboard doors as he got breakfast ready for Miles.

I glanced outside my bedroom window to see Bryce holding a wrench in his hands, and kicking the front tire of his jeep. There was a loud "bang" from the sputtering engine and I smiled to myself, then drifted back to sleep.

Chapter Eight
July

Domestic Diva

> *Dear Diary,*

Drew and I seem to have quickly settled into domestic life. I cook dinner every night, and then he does the dishes. We take turns sharing the computer upstairs while studying, and I usually convince him to watch some American TV with me for half an hour. I want him to have a better understanding of North American culture, although I'm not sure that making him watch *The Apprentice* is helping my cause.

There's another Canadian at school in my program named Andy, an outspoken guy from Calgary who reminds me of a cattle rancher. Andy told me he had heard through the grapevine that I'm "living in sin with two men in Onetai" and that we're always throwing "wild parties" at night. I can understand how the "living in sin" rumor started but the closest thing to a wild party would be watching *Daddy Daycare* on Saturday night with Drew and Miles.

I made some chocolate chip muffins over the weekend and Miles wanted to take some home with him. Drew said I should send some to

Janine, who is back from a recent trip to Melbourne, and that's when I put my foot down.

"No! Are you crazy? There's no way."

"Dah'lin,' we need to set a good example for Miles."

"Drew, you know what…Fine. But don't even think about taking over any of the brownies I made."

There was no point in arguing. I can tell when Drew is feeling determined about something and trying to change his mind is like trying to stop a bull from charging at a red flag. Still, I wish he would respect my wishes not to share my culinary efforts with the enemy.

Stuck in the Middle With Miles

Last night, Miles had a bad dream and couldn't sleep. I pulled myself away from my homework to boil some water for his "hot water teddy". It's actually a hot water Barney, as in, Barney the Dinosaur. The hot water bottle fits inside him.

Miles asked to watch his new Walt Disney video and the next thing I knew, Drew and I were sitting on the couch with Prince Miles happily stretched across our laps, sucking on his thumb and humming to *Pocahontas*.

Janine got back together with her boyfriend and they're in the Cook islands for a week. I think that Drew is overcompensating and needs to be more firm with Miles, even if he misses Janine. Bedtime is bedtime. At least, that's how it was at my house. (Although, the father who enforced my strict curfew is the same father who said I'd be getting a step ladder for an engagement gift, so I can elope. Maybe I'm just jealous).

Drew has finally caved and agreed to my request not to let Miles watch any more violence on TV. I've never thought of myself as a pacifist, but now I understand why all those parents' groups are always up in arms about inappropriate programming.

***

When Miles finally fell asleep, Drew carried him back to his room and we stayed up a bit longer talking on the couch.

"You're a good role model for him, Lindsay. You're going to be a good Mum."

"Thanks. I try."

"I wish Janine was more like you."

I wished Janine would take up permanent residence in Australia, but I kept my thoughts to myself. No point in upsetting the apple cart.

"Thanks."

"I love you."

"I love you too."

Shop 'Til Something Drops

Dear Diary,

This morning, Drew and I attempted the impossible: a three hour shopping trip with Miles. We went to The Warehouse, which is a discount store, similar to Walmart.

Drew and I took turns amusing Miles in the toy aisle while the other person tried to knock things off the shopping list. We needed security lights for the house, a desk for me, a heater, long underwear (for me), and other household items.

Miles was doing well until we got to the cash register and he started to fuss. I bought him some strawberry milk which he was drinking just fine on his own, until Drew said, "Don't drop your milk Miles," which is when he promptly dropped the bottle which splattered all over the floor. When Miles saw Drew's face he started to cry and I wished the floor would swallow me because I had never seen such angry faces as the other shoppers we were standing with.

"People don't realize how hard it is to take care of a three year old," Drew said loudly, to everyone and no one in particular.

"Well Miles, there are going to be consequences for your actions when we get home."

"Yes," I said, trying to sound stern. "There will be consequences."

Several people turned around to stare at me, I assume because they weren't used to hearing an "American" accent.

I somehow doubted there were going to be any real "consequences" but I assumed Drew and I were saying this for the benefit of the other shoppers, as opposed to poor Miles, who had actually done very well for a tired and hungry toddler.

"I want McDonald's," Miles whined.

"Maybe later, Miles."

I was holding him on my hip while Drew paid at the cash register.

A Warehouse staff member came over with a mop and started to clean the floor while shooting dirty looks in our direction.

So this is what family life is really like, I thought. *Interesting.*

Men Are Like Mocha Lattes

I love chocolate. Let me rephrase that. I love all things chocolate, from chocolate mousse, to chocolate chip cookies, to Haagen Daaz Dutch chocolate ice cream. By the time I turned twenty-one, I was an expert in creating chocolate desserts for all occasions, delighting family and friends with black and white chocolate truffles, café brownie sundaes, and chocolate glazed triple-layer cheesecakes. I am a chocoholic. In fact, the only thing I love as much as chocolate is coffee. Starbucks mocha lattes to be exact, although I've been known to settle for a nice cup of white hot chocolate as well, *con panna* (with whipped cream).

It struck me this evening that men are like mocha lattes: a temptation that some of us regret in the morning after indulging the night before. They tend to be available as tall and dark, short and sweet, rich and smooth, non-fat or full-bodied. I think of my ideal man the same way as my favourite latte: tall, non-fat, with deep, rich character. Which begs the question why I'm dating Drew, who isn't tall and doesn't seem to have much depth of character at all. On the other hand, he *is* thin and rich, and he always smells good, so he gets bonus points for aroma. I was feeling homesick last night, so I asked him to take me to Starbucks where I ordered a tall, non-fat mocha latte with extra whipped cream. Drew just looked at me and shook his head. He said the order speaks volumes about North American culture.

Today I kept thinking about Drew's comments, and whether it's true that too many people today want to have their mocha lattes and drink them too. Take Sydney for example: she wants her house and her car, her career, a steady boyfriend and the occasional Friday night fling. She's all about sex with no commitment, even when it means the main guy she's having sex with (in this case, a very lovesick Bryce) is miserable because he can never quite "have" her.

Then there's Drew. He wants to go to school and get his nursing degree, have full custody of Miles and still be able to go for a pint at the pub most nights. I think Drew figured out a while ago that his preferred lifestyle would require a very patient life partner, and his ex-wife Janine certainly didn't fit the bill. She called this morning, to extend her usual invitation to cut my hair.

"Hello?"

"Hello, is this Libby?"

"It's Lindsay."

"Look you Canadian tart, if you don't leave my husband alone, I'm going to drive you straight back to America! I'm going to chop every one of those curls off! Do you hear me? I'm going to—Mum! Mum! Give me back the phone!"

"Hello?" A mature woman's voice on the other end of the line.

"Yes, hello?"

"Who is this?"

"It's Lindsay."

"Who?"

"Lindsay, the Canadian student staying with Drew."

"Oh, *Lindsay*. Yes, of course, Drew's girlfriend. Miles talks about you all the time. Lindsay love, could you be a dear and not ring Janine anymore? It's rather upsetting for her."

"I'm sorry?"

"Janine's father and I would appreciate if you don't call the poor girl. She's been through the wringer with all of Drew's nonsense..."

"But *she's* the one who keeps calling *me*!"

"...really quite upsetting. Well, I must be off. The girls are waiting for me at the country club. We enjoyed your brownies by the way. Good-bye dear."

Click.

I'm going to *kill* Drew. I've told him a million times not to take my desserts over there. I think he tries to placate Janine's family with them, not that it seems to be having the desired effect.

Now, where was I? Right. Having your brownies and eating them too. In Drew's life, the person allowing his mocha latte factor (watching rugby at the pub) is me, the on-site babysitter. I don't mind taking care of Miles at all, in fact, I love spending time with him. But I do wish that Drew would take some responsibility. I worry sometimes about being involved with someone whose only motivations in life seem to be having sex and drinking beer. I have no idea how he manages to take care of his patients at the hospital.

Which brings me to my own mocha latte factor: marriage. The only factor missing from the equation of my life happiness is a husband and a diamond ring to signify my "M.R.S."

I don't think it's asking too much. In the grand scheme of things, my mocha latte factor is a *small*, not a *grande*. Still, it's proving to be as elusive as the proverbial pair of no-run pantyhose.

I think I need to step up my affirmations.

New "Power" Affirmations For This Week
Every day, in every way,
My marriage potential gets better and better
I am a strong, confident, capable woman
I am a goddess
I am a goddess who deserves to snag her Mr. Right

Embracing Your Inner "Desperada"
"How do you say 'desperate' in Spanish?"
"Masculine or feminine?"
"Feminine."
"It's 'desesperada.' I thought you were fluent."
"I can't remember everything."
"Maybe all of that marijuana you smoke has finally affected your memory."
"Very funny."

Sydney took a long drag on her cigarette, forehead furrowed in concentration as she examined her answers to George's latest international languages assignment. We were sitting in the cafeteria, which was almost deserted at 4 pm. A lone caretaker, dressed in a teal polyester uniform with her hair pulled back under a black fishnet cover, was mopping the floors and singing to herself in Maori. Outside, the rain was drumming a steady beat against the windows, the melodic rhythm interrupted now and then by heavy sheets of water that would periodically pummel the high, wooden roof.

"Speaking of 'desesperadas,' Janine called again today."
"What did she say?"
"What didn't she say? I'm an American whore who can't find my own man, so I'm shagging her husband. She'd like to take a hot poker and brand me in the 'arse' with a scarlet 'A.' And if she ever catches Drew

and me in bed together, she's going to take a large pair of scissors and chop my hair off."

"Oh, is that all."

"Mmm…"

"Charming. Is she still planning to drive you back to America?"

"She says she's going to drive all of us out of Drew's flat after she's made our lives a living hell."

"Sounds like she's the one whose life is a living hell."

"She phoned *six times* this morning! It's like she has nothing better to do with her time."

"What does Bryce say when she calls?"

"He doesn't answer the phone anymore."

"That sounds like Bryce," Sydney laughed.

"How are things going with him, anyway?"

"With Bryce? Oh, I don't know. He's sweet."

"Sweet as in, you love it when he brings you flowers, or sweet as in, you really have no interest in him?"

"I like it when he brings me flowers."

"And…?"

"And he's good in bed. What else can I say?"

"Sydney! The poor guy is head over heels in love with you!"

"So?"

"So, don't you think you at least owe him a chance?"

"Lindsay, I'm shagging him. What more can a bloke ask for?"

"He's *in love* with you!"

"And he still flirts with *you*!"

"I hope you don't think I'm interested in him. I think it's just an act."

"What I think, is that Bryce is desperate to get married, just like you. You're two peas in a pod."

"I'm not desperate."

"*No estas desesperada Señorita? Yo no lo creo.*"

"Well, believe it. I'm not a 'desperada'."

"Desesperada."

"Thank you, Professor Higgins. Who's the one who just taught you that?"

"Oooh! Touché, my Fair Lady," she replied, leaning back in her chair with a grin.

"Seriously Sydney, I'm not desperate. I do have standards. I'm not just going to marry the first guy on the street who asks me."

"So what if Drew asks you?"

"Drew? We're not even dating."

"No, you're just living together, shagging and taking care of a three-year old. You're right, it sounds like a lot more than dating to me," she said, smiling mischievously.

"Sydney! Stop pushing my buttons!"

"You're right. I should leave that to Drew. I bet he knows exactly which 'buttons' to *push.*" Sydney threw her head back and laughed, auburn curls shaking, loud peals of laughter ringing through the cafeteria. The caretaker glanced over at our table with her eyebrows raised, then shook her head, and went back to mopping the floor.

"I'm glad you amuse you."

"Is that a smile I see at the corners of your mouth? Is *Señorita* Lindsay trying not to laugh?"

"Sydney, you're terrible. You're worse than Janine."

"Lindsay, I love you. You're too sweet."

"You know, I think Janine really does hate me."

"There's a surprise."

"What do you mean?"

"Of course she hates you. You're having sex with her husband."

"Ex-husband."

"Is the divorce final yet?"

"As of this week."

"Really!" Sydney sat back in her chair, and slowly exhaled a ring of smoke from her mouth.

"Well, well. Looks like you and Drew have some celebrating to do."

"I don't want to celebrate. I actually feel sorry for her."

"Why should you feel sorry for her? She's been driving you mad ever since you got here!"

"I know. I just don't feel right about celebrating the end of her marriage."

"Jesus, Lindsay. You're incredible. You leave this cushy job in Toronto..."

"I hated my job in Toronto."

"You leave Toronto to come all the way to New Zealand, where you land in a hornet's nest…"

"I wouldn't exactly call it a hornet's nest. I mean, Drew and I have a lot of fun sometimes…"

"When he's not at the pub or sitting in front of the telly watching rugby. Has he ever stood up for you when Janine rings or comes 'round the house to make her threats?"

"He's…you know what? I think he's a pacifist."

"Do you actually believe what you just said?"

"What? Of course I do."

"Lindsay, you know what your trouble is? You're more concerned about everyone else than you are about yourself."

We looked at each other in silence for a few moments, listening to the sound of the rain as it continued to pelt against the windows. Sydney took a final drag on her cigarette, then let the butt drop to the floor, and ground it out with her heel. I turned my head to see whether the caretaker had noticed, but she was still singing away, oblivious to the damage Sydney had just done to her freshly mopped floor.

"Well, I better get going." I stood up, brushing ham and cheese pie crumbs from my lap.

"Thanks for lunch."

"Lindsay, you aren't cross with me, are you? I'm on your side. Why do you think I had that talk with our friend George? You're passing his class with flying colors now."

"That's because you convinced him to let us be partners, and you hand in all the work. He still hates me."

"He doesn't hate you. He's a stroppy old bugger who doesn't like Americans."

"I'm Canadian."

"Lindsay…" Sydney sighed deeply as though my words pained her. "Sometimes you have to accept people the way they are. You can't change them."

"I'm not trying to change George. I'm trying to make him see that I'm a good person."

"George doesn't care if you're a good person. All George cares about are politics and being the boss in his classroom. The rest is irrelevant."

"Anyway, I'm going." I pulled my umbrella out of my knapsack, still damp from when I had used it earlier.

"Lindsay, you're still cross."

"Do you really think I'm 'desperate'?" I asked, putting my knapsack back down on the table.

"What's wrong with being desperate? I'm always desperate for something: sex, a cigarette..."

"So, the answer is 'yes.'"

"The answer is, we're *all* desperate for something. Everyone. I bet you're desperate for one of your orange vodka coolers right now, to take your mind off things."

"That's different."

"How?"

"There's a difference between wanting an orange vodka cooler, and wanting to get married. My life happiness doesn't depend on a vodka cooler."

"So, your life happiness depends on getting married?"

"Yes."

"And what if it doesn't happen?"

"If it doesn't happen? It has to happen."

"Or what?"

"Or I'll—I don't know. Look Sydney, I have to go."

"Lindsay, I'm sorry. I don't mean to upset you. I just don't understand how such a beautiful girl, with so much going for her, can be so *miserable* over a stupid piece of paper."

"It isn't just the piece of paper. It's the whole idea of being in love, having romance and friendship in my life..."

"You had that with your ex didn't you?"

"Who, Ben? Yeah, I guess you could say that. But it wasn't the same."

"Why not?"

"God, I don't know, a million different reasons. His family was never as friendly to me as they were to his brother's wives. His sister could never remember my name. His parents used to make us sleep in separate bedrooms at the cottage..."

"You're joking. Didn't the two of you live together?"

"For the last couple of years."

"His family sounds barmy."

"Well, anyway. I always felt like an outsider. It was like, in their eyes, I didn't count if I wasn't married to him."

"So you wanted recognition."

"Mmm..."

"Lindsay, that's normal. Look, Ben is in the past. Drew's family recognizes you, don't they? Didn't his grandma give you that necklace you're wearing?"

I glanced down at the blue glass cameo around my neck.

"Yeah."

"Cheer up, Lindsay. Things could be worse. You're spending the year in New Zealand, you're having hot sex with a good-looking Kiwi..."

"I'm homesick, I have allergies, I don't like teacher's college..."

"Lindsay, you're impossible. Come on. I'm taking you out for a pint."

"So, beer is the answer to all of life's problems?"

"Stop being such a party pooper. It'll be fun."

Sydney pressed her lips together, having applied a fresh coat of mulberry gloss to them. "Ok!" She announced, standing up.

"Let's hand this assignment in to George, head to The Pump, and find some good-looking blokes. I'm in *desperate* need of a proper thumping!" And with that, she dissolved into peals of laughter again, as I shook my head and followed her out the cafeteria door.

Desesperada, indeed.

Flirt and Convert

Dear Diary,

I'm homesick. Drew is at work and Bryce is out for the evening. I bought myself a copy of *Who* magazine, which is the closest thing here to *In Touch* or *Us Weekly*. The headlines this week read:

Kirsty Alley: I don't like the way that I look but I like who I am.
Mary-Kate Olsen: Back home but still battling anorexia.
Hugh Grant: Caught! Out with Jemima.
Nick Talks: Why I split with Paris.

I wish I was Paris Hilton right now. I bet she's never had to spend the night home alone.

7:30 pm

Why did Gwyneth Paltrow name her daughter "Apple"? I feel sorry for the girl.

8:05 pm

Britney Spears is engaged to someone called "Kevin Federline." He reminds me of Not Good Looking at All from the airport in Fiji. I guess I'll never know whether he made it to his wedding.

8:07 pm

I love these Kiwi "goss" magazines. There's an article called, "Gwyneth Paltrow—Mad for Organics!" Her rep denied the story. (Although, this could explain the whole "Apple" thing.)

8:40 pm

I wonder if Drew really used to sing in the church choir as he claims, or if he was just trying to impress me? One thing I've never understood is why he insists he's a born-again Christian when,

a) He slept with Janine, (who isn't even a Christian), before getting married. This resulted in a shot-gun wedding. I told him that's the danger when you try to flirt and convert.

b) Drew is the one who mounted the campaign for us to sleep together—while he was still technically married.

c) I'm the one who drags everyone to church twice a month.

It's hard to look the Pastor in the eye when he says "Good morning" and shakes my hand. Drew is completely unfazed. I have a hard time believing he was actually a choir boy. Hmmm…

11:00 pm

Drew phoned to say he'll be home in an hour. He also said he has a surprise for me. I still wish I could trade places with Paris Hilton for the evening.

Love Means Never Having To Say You're Married

"Sweets, are you awake? Sweets?"

"I am now!" I rolled over in bed, to see Drew's face inches away from me, new stubble just beginning to darken his features. I could smell the faint spice of his new cologne still fragrant on his T-shirt, and felt a tickling sensation in my nose.

"Drew, you have to stop using that—that—A-CHOO!" Drew pulled away with a grimace, not quite escaping a light shower of phlegm.

"Shivers! Lindsay, we have to get you something better for those allergies. Goodness me."

"Ugh. I feel like I just woke from the dead. What time is it?"

I looked around the room, feeling disoriented. The morning light wasn't quite warm, but the rays filtering through the pale green curtains on the windows were bright, and filled the airy bedroom with the promise of a fresh day—one that I wasn't ready to begin just yet.

"It's not quite seven."

"Seven *am?* It's only seven o'clock in the morning? Why did you wake me up? It's Saturday!"

"Sweets, I have a surprise for you."

"Oh, no…that's what you said last night!"

"You're so cheeky! Just wait there."

"Believe me, I'm not going anywhere except back to sleep!"

I reached under my pillow and found my black satin sleep mask, then put it over my eyes and rolled away from the door, planning to get another couple of hours of rest.

Five minutes later, as I was drifting off into the clouds of a delicious dream, I heard Drew's voice suddenly boom inches away from me, jolting me wide awake again.

"Sweets!"

"What is it?" I shouted, losing my patience.

"Dammit Drew—I'm tired! You can't keep me up all night with sexual gymnastics and then expect me to just…oh."

I was now sitting straight up in bed, and could see that Drew had prepared a breakfast tray for me. There were fried banana slices, homemade French toast, and coffee with what smelled like coconut cream. In the center of the tray was a single red rose in a crystal vase, and a small envelope with my name written on it in calligraphy.

"Wow, Drew. I'm sorry. This is—wow."

"I got you real maple syrup as well."

Drew took his hand from behind his back where he had hidden it, and showed me a glass container of syrup with a red maple leaf on it.

"All the way from Canada."

"Where did you get it?" I stared at him in amazement, wondering what was going on.

"I got it from your Mum. I asked her to send it to me in the post."

"How did...never mind. When did you call my..."

"Open the card."

Drew was smiling at me, eyes dancing with excitement.

I tore the side of the envelope, and took out a card with a red heart on the cover.

"You know my birthday isn't until November, right?"

"Just open it!"

Slowly, I opened the card to see one word written in bold, black calligraphy:

"Downstairs."

"Is Bryce up yet?"

"He told me he's staying with Sydney for the weekend."

"Where's Miles?"

"He's with his grandparents for the weekend. They're bringing him back on Sunday night. You're all mine today!"

Drew scooped me up in his arms, and fit my sleep mask back over my eyes.

"What about breakfast? It's going to get cold! Drew! Make sure you don't bang my head on the doorway!"

Thirty seconds later, I was standing in the living room, sleep mask still around my eyes, shivering in the filmy white negligee that Drew had bought me from the new French lingerie store in town.

"Can I look?"

"Yes."

I felt Drew's breath against my neck, as he slipped off my sleep mask, and wrapped his arms around me in a tight embrace from behind.

"Oh my God!"

"What do you think?"

"Oh my God! Drew!"

The kitchen and living room had been transformed into an oasis of red roses and white candles. There were large bouquets everywhere, and Drew had covered the kitchen table with a white cloth, covered in rose petals. Two magnolia-scented candles burned at opposite ends of the table, and in the middle was a framed picture of Drew and me, taken during our visit to Helena's house at Easter. A blue velvet box stood in front of the silver picture frame.

I felt like I still hadn't woken up yet, and literally pinched myself to make sure I wasn't dreaming.

"Go ahead...open the box."

I reached over and snapped open the top of the box, holding my breath. There, nestled amongst crushed velvet, was a beautifully cut, radiant diamond set in yellow gold.

Drew gently took the box from my hand, and his right leg stepped behind as he lowered it to the ground, while I watched in complete amazement.

"Lindsay Breyer..."

"Oh my God." I exhaled, feeling tears well in my eyes.

"I love you. Will you marry me?"

A million thoughts flooded my mind, as I stood, watching this handsome man down on bended knee, offering me an engagement ring.

Why did I have to be such a bitch this morning? How am I going to tell this story to my friends now? Where did he manage to hide all these roses? Do I have sleep in my eyes? God! I can't believe that—

"Lindsay?"

"Sorry! Drew—I—I'm overwhelmed. I just—yes! Yes, of course I'll marry you!"

Drew slipped the ring on my wedding finger, then swept me off my feet in a huge bear hug, while both of us laughed.

"Right then. Let's have breakfast together in bed shall we?"

"Sounds good to me. I'll help you blow these candles out."

"And then we'll get that sleep mask back on you!" he said, slapping my rear end.

"Drew! You're terrible!"

"Terribly, madly in love with you."

"So, when will we have the wedding?"

"Aw, we can talk about that later Sweets. You're not fussed about that, are you? We're in love, we don't have to be married next week!"

"No, I guess not."

"Are you happy?"

"I'm very happy. I couldn't ask for anything more right now."

"I'll call Mum this evening to tell her the news. I expect she'll want to come 'round with my Grandma to celebrate sometime soon."

"Mmm...there's so much to do!"

"The only thing I want to think about doing right now is *you!*"

"Drew! This is supposed to be a romantic moment."

"It's about to get very romantic..."

***

Lindsay,

Congratulations on the engagement. Are you happy now? Hope that guy's ex doesn't snap and chop all your hair off.

I wasn't home when you called, had a blind date with a girl from Lavalife. Turned out the photo she posted was about ten years old. Actually, I'm not even sure it was her.

Anyway, Mom and Dad have already been to the travel agent to look into the cost of airfare to New Zealand. When's the wedding?

Take care and watch your back,

Nathan

Dear Nathan,

Thanks for the concern, but I don't think Janine is actually going to chop my hair off. Drew says she's been taking the news well, actually. She's too caught up in her new romance to notice much else. As long as we can look after Miles for her on the weekend, I think she'll be fine.

No date yet for the wedding. We'll probably have it early next year, there's no real rush.

We're in love, and we're engaged and I have the most beautiful diamond ring! I'll keep you posted on the plans.

Love,

Lindsay

Chapter Nine

August

Dear Diary,

I can't sleep. Drew and I had a huge fight today. I was angry because he cancelled our plans for lunch together. Janine called him at the last minute, asking him to take care of Miles for a few hours because she wanted to get her nails done. Of course, he gave in to her. I told him I wouldn't tolerate this happening anymore, and he said I better get used to it, because he doesn't plan on making an enemy of his ex. I told him it isn't making an enemy of his ex to set boundaries with her, but he brushed off my concerns. Then he had the audacity to say that I'm not the "girl that he proposed to" because that person isn't a "selfish, self-absorbed princess"! I was furious, and flung my engagement ring at him. He barely reacted, just said he was putting it on the dresser and that I could wear it again when I've finished my "temper tantrum". Oooooh! He makes my blood boil. I told him that I think we need to take a "break" from each other and he said, "fine". So...*fine.*

11:00 pm

I hate New Zealand. I hate, loathe and despise this weather. It's cold and damp, and I am freezing to death in this bed. Why doesn't anyone have central heat?

11:15 pm

I hate Drew. I hate, loathe and despise Kiwi men. I am thinking of moving to Tibet and giving up on the opposite sex forever.

11:55 pm

I can't sleep. This is terrible. I'm going to wake up with dark circles under my eyes, and Drew will know that I was upset. Damn him. I hope Janine takes him for everything he's worth. No, wait—why should she enjoy all of his family's money when I'm the one who's been supporting him for the past six months? I'm the one who should be getting alimony.

12:10 am

Come to think of it, I should be getting alimony.

12:23 am

The truth is, I'm too good for him. His own mother said that he has "baggage". And sure, his family has millions of dollars, but by the time he ever inherited any of it, we'd be too old to enjoy it. Yolanda doesn't seem as though she's going anywhere for a while and Helena would probably live to be 150, just to spite me.

1:40 am

This is the worst trip of my entire life.

2:00 am

I am an idiot. I just emailed Avery, an old ex. Now he knows that I've been thinking about him eighteen months after our break-up. His ego will be swelling so much, there won't be any oxygen left for the rest of Canada to breathe. God—I hate this trip.

2:45 am

OK. I have a plan. I'll marry Bryce. It's perfect. Drew will be jealous and miserable for the rest of his life, and I'll be the happy daughter-in-law of Bryce's parents who are apparently a lot nicer than Helena anyway.

3:00 am

I just burned my tongue trying to drink a cup of hot milk. I left it in the microwave too long. I can't do anything right. I'm almost thirty-years-old and I'm still not married. While all my friends at home are snuggled up with their husbands, watching the season finale of *Sex and the City*, I am freezing to death in a foreign country on the other side of the world—alone.

I'm tempted to call Janine—payback for all the times she's woken me up or otherwise bothered me at midnight—but no, better not. I'm not sure who I hate more right now, her or Drew.

Her.

Drew.

Her.

No, Drew.

OK, I hate them both equally.

4:07 am

I should join a convent. One day, someone, maybe Sydney, maybe Nathan, will write a book about my life: *The Tragic Demise of the One Girl from High School Who Truly Deserved to Be Married.* The book will have lots of photographs so that readers can see that I'm not hideously ugly, and that it really is possible for such a hideous thing (perpetual singlehood) to happen.

They could get the Church of Latter Day Saints to do a commercial. The actress playing me would be standing forlornly outside the window of Helena's living room, watching Miles open his Christmas presents while Drew drinks a cup of tea and chuckles, arm around another woman's shoulders. The voice over would say:

"Don't get left out in the cold. If you think you can do better than the cute bartender you met after graduating from high school, think again. This girl thought she could do better."

And there would be a close-up of a tear rolling down my, I mean the actress's cheek, as she reflects on how she is doomed to be dumped by one boyfriend after another, and watch them move on with their lives without a passing thought about her.

The voice over would continue:

"When Lindsay Breyer was eighteen, she thought she had all the time in the world to find a husband. She was wrong. After her last boyfriend left her for another woman, Lindsay was arrested for stalking him and his new family, by New Zealand police. Today, Lindsay lives in a convent with other nuns who also thought they could do better.

Don't let this happen to you. Marry the first person who asks. If you think you can do better, just remember, you can't."

Well, something like that.

Seriously though, they should warn young women about these things. I'm going to write a letter to Oprah.

5:00 am

Avery responded to my email. Now what?

Dear Lindsay,

I've been wondering where you are. What the hell are you doing at teacher's college? You're a lawyer.

No, I'm not going to use my influence to get you an Ambassadorship like Angelina Jolie. You should have thought about what you were giving up eighteen months ago.

I hope you think about getting a serious job when you come home. I do think about our relationship sometimes, but when I become Prime Minister, I need a mature woman beside me, not a sulky teen-ager who complains about petty things, like not being introduced to Bono.

The Senator doesn't think you're the right person for me. He says you don't know what you want.

Do you?

-A

Dear Avery,

Thanks for reminding me why I broke up with you.

Lindsay

P.S. If you ever do become Prime Minister, I will renounce my citizenship.

7 am

I am so upset, I just ate three Magnum ice cream bars. The dairy owner must think I'm some kind of binge eater, which apparently, I am. I also bought a copy of *Who* magazine, even though I've promised myself not to spend any more money supporting the "cult of celebrity worship".

Time to get some sleep.

Early Morning Affirmations

I am a brave, confident, capable woman

I am a goddess

I am a goddess who's…at least still engaged.

Chapter Ten

September - Part 1
Looking for Mr. Right
or
The Modern Day Search for the Holy Grail

Looking For Mr. Right
Or,
The Modern Day Search for the Holy Grail
by Lindsay Breyer

Love is all around us, so the song goes. But if you're anything like me, a single, almost thirty-year old who's short on (biological) time and long on lonely Saturday nights in front of the TV, finding love can feel more elusive than finding a pair of pantyhose that won't run.

Hope springs eternal, so we peruse the bookstores, pretending to browse the latest fashion magazines while keeping a watchful eye on the self-help section. As soon as the coast is clear, we make a break for it, filling our arms with books from the relationship shelf at lightning speed. Now is not the time to be seen by an ex-boyfriend, or worse, an ex-girlfriend sporting a shiny diamond ring (which she will conspicuously wave in your face while you are expected to offer your congratulations).

The book titles you find are discomfiting:

Why There Are No Good Men Left: The Plight of the New Single Woman;

Why Men Marry Bitches;

The Surrendered Single.

None of these strike you as particularly hopeful, yet curiously, they are not as depressing as *The Kama Sutra for Sexy Couples.* Of course, after reading, oh, about twenty of these books, you will find yourself more confused than if you attempted to take a calculus class in a foreign language.

There are *Rules* that promote deception and scheming as the best way to convince a man of your sense of self-worth. So, if a man phones you on Wednesday night for a date on Saturday, you must tell him you're busy, even if he was trying to surprise you with concert tickets that he just scored through work. Even if it's your favorite band playing the concert. Even if you'll now spend Saturday night alone while your boyfriend watches your favorite band in concert with that cute receptionist from the fifth floor. *She's just a good friend,* he'll insist. *You can't make it Sweetie, you don't expect me to go alone, now do you?*

But wait—what if he asked you to the concert on a *Tuesday?* You're not off the hook yet *Señorita,* because now you have to calculate whether you've been maintaining the correct ratio of accepting and turning down dates: you should only accept two thirds of his invitations. This is because your boyfriend is a *man,* and therefore from another planet. The thrill of the chase is the only reason that he's interested in you. What, you may ask, happens if a miracle occurs and you actually do get married? How do you keep up the charade of pretending to be busy then? Logically, if the man can see you every night, or three thirds of the time instead of only two thirds, he will still lose interest and suddenly find the cute receptionist on the fifth floor a more challenging prey. Do you adapt the rules, along the lines of, "Not tonight Dear, I have a headache"?

Unfortunately, I do not have the answer, being a single, never-married woman myself. But, I'd venture to guess that the *Rules Ladies* have their own devious advice for legal couplehood as well. Of course, if you're not a *Rules* kind of person, you can certainly find a wealth of advice from the other "experts," that is, anyone who's married or has been married, and therefore knows far more about these matters than single old you.

There are authors who advocate meditation and affirmations as the best way to manifest *The One*; there are authors who advocate open and honest communication. Others suggest more dire measures, such as breaking up with a commitment-phobic boyfriend to prove a point. The metaphors are disconcerting; for example, there's "sealing the deal". In the language of sales, some of us are "great openers", that is, able to find and keep a man for months or even years, yet sadly unable to close the transaction. And, these Deal Closing authors insist, this is all about sales work: selling yourself as a high-priced commodity that won't be on the shelf forever.

In summary, you would find simpler and more consistent advice if you asked a group of ten people the best way to stop a fit of hiccups. The question is, do any of the strategies actually work? Well, all we know for sure is that they seem to work for the authors who pocket lots of cash for promoting them. It almost gives you fresh determination to marry, if for no other reason than to win the legitimacy to write and sell your own books on the topic.

Truth be told, the bookstore can be a comforting place where you might spend your time browsing selections of reading material with other human beings, instead of at home alone with your cat. Unless of course, it's Valentine's Day, in which case I personally advise avoiding the malls altogether. You will also want to avoid all newspapers and magazines, which will be full of the latest statistics about how married couples are healthier, wealthier, and happier than you. Superior, really, is what the researchers are saying. It's a bit like encouraging a four year old to help himself to a slice of chocolate cake, placed six inches out of reach. Sadistic. Given the option, most of us would blissfully disappear into married *Never Never Land*. But first, we need Peter Pan.

As far as all of the complicated schemes to snag a man, I still think that honesty is the best policy, that friendship should be at the heart of it all, and that you should always say "yes" to seeing your favorite band in concert, even if someone asks you a half hour before the show starts. I believe that true love flourishes when two people stop playing games, and start seeing each other as flawed, but still lovable, human beings. Like wearing mini-skirts after thirty, some "rules" need to be broken.

***

"Well, what do you think? Do you like it?"

I had just finished reading Drew the rough draft of an article I planned to submit to *Elle Magazine*.

He was sitting on the bed in his boxer shorts, absent-mindedly scratching Tigger behind the ears.

"Is it supposed to be funny?"

"What do you mean 'Is it supposed to be funny?' Of *course* it's supposed to be funny!"

"I think Janine used *The Rules* before we got married."

"Uh huh. I thought you had a shot-gun wedding."

"I reckon *The Rules* aren't that bad."

"Mmm hmm. Anything else?"

"You don't spend your nights alone with the cat."

Tigger looked up at him, and reached a paw out to bat at his leg with an annoyed "meow".

"I know. I'm just using some creative license."

"But we're engaged. Why are you writing about being single?"

"Because..."

I paused for a moment, as I realized that I wasn't really single anymore. On the other hand, I wasn't married either. I was in a hazy twilight zone, somewhere between frozen dinners in front of the TV alone, and saying, "Not tonight Dear, I have a headache." Interesting.

"Well, technically I'm still single. There's no official status for being engaged."

"But it sounds like you're still looking for Mr. Right."

A long silence.

"Well...that's the point. I've been looking for Mr. Right for the past ten years. So I can identify with all the women who still are."

"Why don't you write about being engaged, and planning our wedding? Something cheerful, eh?"

"Because I just spent six hours writing *this*!"

I grabbed my article from his hands, and stomped down the stairs.

"Sweets, I'm only trying to be helpful!" Drew called down after me.

I found Bryce at the kitchen table, spreading strawberry jam on toast, and took a seat across from him.

"Trouble in paradise?" he asked with a smirk on his face.

"Wouldn't *you* love to know?"

"I wouldn't, actually. Toast?" He held out a piece of a slightly charred whole wheat bagel.

"Sure, I guess."

We sat at the table in silence for a few moments, listening to the clock tick.

"You know," he said, looking at me with cautious hope, "You'd like me if you really got to know me."

"Bryce..." I glanced at the stairs, but didn't see Drew who had turned on the radio in the bedroom.

"How's Sydney these days?" I asked, trying to change the subject.

"Wouldn't know." He let his knife fall to the plate with a small clatter, and looked at me challengingly.

"Well, I better get going," I said breezily (at least, I was trying to sound light and breezy). I got up from the table to put my dishes away, wishing I had found a place with female roommates.

"Can I read this?" He was holding my article in his left hand and I could see he had already managed to smudge some strawberry jam on it.

"Go ahead. But I don't want to hear any negative criticism!"

"I'd never criticize you," he said, opening his eyes wide.

"Right!" I laughed, shaking my head. "Have a good day Bryce."

"Do you need a ride?"

"No thanks. I'll see you later. Tell Drew that I've gone to do some window shopping."

Soap Gets in Your Eyes

When Drew and I made love for the first time, it was so perfect, we could have been in a movie. Unfortunately, six months later, things aren't quite as romantic. I have no one to blame but myself. Drew woke up before me and brought me breakfast in bed again: a fruit smoothie, eggs, toast and fried banana. I was impressed. Then, I had the brilliant idea for us to have a shower together.

Drew told me to go ahead and start running the water, while he looked for fresh towels. When he joined me, I realized there wasn't as much room as I had thought because of the ceiling that slopes down across the bathtub. I had cleared Miles' toys out of the way, as well as the Johnson's baby shampoo that I got him because he was always getting soap in his eyes and crying when Drew washes his hair.

We took turns lathering each other with a bar of Bryce's Irish Spring, and then Drew lowered himself to his knees to kiss my stomach. I placed both of my hands on his head which was covered with shampoo, and they slipped from his forehead to his face, getting soap inside his eyes.

"Drew! I'm so sorry...are you OK?"

"Yup, yup."

Drew had stood up and was blindly trying to reach for the towel on the bathroom counter. I handed it to him, and suggested that we dry ourselves off but he had other plans in mind. The water began to turn cold and I started to wish I had never suggested having a shower. What was I thinking? These things are never as romantic in real life as they are in the movies...

Drew decided to lift me in the air and I wrapped my legs around his waist, warning him to be careful that my head didn't get banged on the ceiling.

Sure enough, I banged my head on the ceiling.

"Ouch! Drew, put me down!"

"Sweets! Are you okay? Are you alright dah'lin'?"

I was still surprised from the hurt and in too much pain to be gracious.

"No! I'm not okay! My head is killing me! And I'm freezing!"

"Ahem."

We both looked at each other as Bryce cleared his throat outside the door.

"Sorry to bother. Are you going to be much longer?"

"Yes!"

"Sweets! Let me fetch you a towel from the clothesline, and you can rest for a bit."

Drew had wrapped the only towel in the bathroom around his waist and was about to open the door.

"Shall I fetch you a towel, Sweets?" called Bryce.

Wonderful, just wonderful. It isn't enough for me to suffer pain, I have to suffer both pain and humiliation in the same morning. I'm sure there's a lesson in this somewhere...

Frieda's Finishing School

Today was my first day at Frieda's Finishing School. I arrived late, incurring the wrath of Frieda, a matronly woman with short, grey hair and glasses, who looks like she's in her mid-fifties.

I had tried to wake up for 7 am. I told Drew to set the alarm the night before, but for some reason he refuses to. He prefers to wake up "naturally" and tells me that I worry too much. Monday mornings are tricky because Miles is usually here with us. The men of the house do not see the need for a bathroom schedule, which means that everyone ends up trying to take a shower at the same time. Someone is always standing in the kitchen wearing nothing but a towel which makes me feel like I'm living in a hostel in Amsterdam. Thankfully, Miles is easy to deal with. He's happy to sit and watch cartoons while eating his cereal in the living room.

After getting up, I stood in my pyjamas for twenty minutes waiting for Bryce to finish his shower, only to discover there was no hot water left when he finally came out. Drew insisted on cooking breakfast because he's convinced that I'm anorexic. Ever since the curried chicken episode, he's been leaving brochures on my night table with titles like, *What To Do If You Think You Might Have An Eating Disorder.* I have given up trying to explain my crazy metabolism. He insisted on making me a fried egg sandwich and coffee with coconut cream, which I ignored while grabbing a semi-wet towel from the clothes line outside after discovering that Bryce had used mine.

Five minutes later, hair wet and teeth chattering, I was trying to put on a new pair of pantyhose, only to find that they ran as soon as I got into them. I yanked them off, and tried to find another pair in Drew's sock drawer, while he called from downstairs to tell me it was ten to eight and we were going to be late if I didn't hurry. Panicking, I ran down the stairs holding a wrinkled pair of pants, which I begged Drew to iron while I tried to fix my hair which was a tangled mess because I hadn't used any conditioner. He told me that my coffee was getting cold and that he didn't want me leaving the house without eating breakfast.

Bryce was eating his own breakfast at the kitchen table, and grinning to himself while he finished a homework assignment. I was standing at the bottom of the stairs in a pair of Drew's boxer shorts, and a white T-shirt that didn't leave much to the imagination. I still hadn't found time to buy a bathrobe which only contributed to the whole "Sodom and Gomorrah" atmosphere inside the house.

"Drew! I don't think you're grasping the situation! I'm going to be late for my first day of classes! Please help me."

"OK, Gorgeous. But I want you to eat the sandwich in the car."

"Thank you!"

I ran back upstairs while Bryce dryly commented about someone "being whipped" and I thought, *Great. That's just what I need on top of everything else: someone planting ideas inside my boyfriend's head.*

Fifteen minutes later, we were finally in the car on the way to the school. My sandwich was balanced on my lap while I put my make-up on using the mirror in my passenger seat. Miles was sucking his thumb, dried tears on his cheeks, singing "Five little ducks". He had cried when we told him we had to turn the TV off and Drew finally had to bribe him with a cookie. Then he wouldn't come unless he had his Paddington Bear. He kept pulling Paddington's string to make him say "Please take care of this bear" and it wasn't long before my head was aching.

I had no idea how I was going to compose myself after such a circus. As we pulled into the school parking lot, Miles perked up.

"It's Lindsay's work! Can I go with Lindsay?"

"Not now, Miles. That's a good boy."

"But I want to go with Lindsay!"

Miles started to cry and threw his Paddington Bear out the car window. I saw the school receptionist staring at us through the glass windows of the front office, and quickly got out of the car, grabbed Paddington, and gave him to Miles who I kissed on the cheek. I promised to make him some chocolate chip cookies later in the week, which seemed to console him.

"Lindsay. You didn't eat your breakfast." Drew had a reproachful expression on his face, but I was in too much of a hurry to feel guilty.

"I know. I'm sorry. I'll see you this afternoon. Love you!"

And that is how I came to be sitting in Frieda's office, trying to explain my tardiness on my first day of classes. I was only five minutes late but she has a very strict sign-in policy, monitored by another receptionist at the staff entrance. I promised her that it would not happen again. She looked at the huge purple bump on my forehead and asked me what had happened.

"Hmm? You mean this little thing? I—well, I accidentally hit my forehead in the shower," I said, turning a bright shade of red at the memory. Frieda peered at me suspiciously over her glasses and asked whether I was quite alright.

"Quite. Yes. I'm fine."

I was relieved when she finally let me proceed to the staff room, where I found the other student teachers.

My stomach rumbled, and I wished that I had brought Drew's sandwich with me. I was surprised at how formal everything seemed, although I suppose it was to be expected given the prestige of the school. I was given a time schedule and saw that I had mainly French classes with "Shane" as well as a few drama classes with "Eileen".

Chris, another student teacher, walked me to the International Languages Department and I realized that once again, most of the students were taller than me as we passed them in the corridors, although they were all female and wearing navy blue school uniforms. Chris is about six feet tall and gangly, with dark hair, freckles, and thick-rimmed glasses. He told me he was from the University of Auckland and assured me it is far more prestigious than Tutage Teacher's College.

He offered me a "jaffa" and I took the red candy, and wondered again why Aucklanders are called "jaffas" outside of the city. It's a Maori expression, and not a complimentary one. I think it translates into something like, "Pretentious city bastards," only more vulgar.

Once inside the Languages Department, a portable near the back of the school campus, I was introduced to Shane, my "form teacher". He looks exactly like my grade eleven French teacher, Mr. Yashar, but without the glasses: tall, bald, and wearing an expression that's somehow both amused and bewildered at the same time.

I was also introduced to Connie, a tired-looking woman in her forties who later told me in private that she would soon be leaving for Thailand because she was disgusted with the shenanigans that went on at the department. She didn't actually use the word "shenanigans" but I understood her meaning.

Connie gave a farewell speech a week later, in which she lambasted Shane and the department head (also a man) while describing how the two interrogated her daily about who was "staying on top" of whom in the International Languages Department, from the time of her arrival. It was a clever speech, and seemed to produce the desired effect of causing the department head some anxiety as his own speech fluttered in his trembling right hand. Men!

Greasy Business

This evening I couldn't bear the thought of staying home alone. The frigid temperature is beyond bearable and when Drew works at night, there's no extra body heat in the bed to keep me warm. Drew had been saving a coupon for The Sheraton that he found in the newspaper, and suggested that I go, his treat. He didn't have to ask me twice, although it would have made more sense for him to spend the money on proper heating for the house.

As soon as I had been shown my room, I turned up the heat and had a long, hot shower. Then I turned on the TV and had a look at the room service menu. We haven't exactly been eating the healthiest food at home. Drew made me bread pudding the other night and it was good, but between the bread pudding and fish and chips that we have when I'm not making tuna casserole, I can't remember the last time I had a fresh fruit or vegetable. Bryce did the shopping the other night and predictably came back with things like sausages, mustard, potato chips and beer. He told me that produce is too expensive.

I called room service and asked them if they could suggest something healthy to eat, because I could only find things like hamburgers and French fries on the menu. The woman on the other end of the line put me through to the kitchen. I explained to the cook that I was looking for something healthy to eat, and wondered if he could recommend anything. I also mentioned that I was homesick. I'm not sure what I was asking for really, maybe a plate of French toast with maple syrup and some fruit salad with cottage cheese.

"You're American!" the cook exclaimed.

"You want pizza, French fries, you want grease Miss!"

"No, no, the opposite. I want something HEALTHY!"

I can't understand why it's so hard to make myself understood sometimes. I'm never sure whether people are pulling my leg, having trouble understanding my "accent," or misunderstanding my expressions. Maybe it's all of the above.

In the end, I had stir-fried vegetables and noodles for dinner, which was perfect.

It was a relief to have the room to myself and enjoy the peace and quiet. No phone ringing off the hook, no loud music blaring from two different rooms at the same time as the living room TV, and no crying toddler to attend to.

Drew came to visit me for an hour and we had a bath together. He was excited to make love in the king-sized bed and saw it as an opportunity to try some new positions.

I had been running on three hours of sleep for the past four nights as I tried to finish assignments, and wasn't up to bedroom gymnastics.

"Sweetie, we'll try the new positions this weekend. I promise. I just want to make love the way we usually do and go to sleep."

"Miles is with us on the weekend."

"Ok, then we'll find time tomorrow afternoon before he gets there."

"Sweets, there won't be time after I pick you up from school."

"Ok, can we just get under the covers and see what happens?"

"You know what will happen. I got this room for us to have some quality time together!"

"So we can recreate a scene from one of Bryce's DVDs that you think I don't know you watch?"

"You're so cheeky."

"I know. Here's my cheek."

He laughed and we finally settled into our routine. Or so I thought.

"Mmm...that feels good. You're amazing. Mmm...that's perfect. Don't stop. Wait...Drew, why are you stopping?"

"I want you to sit on top of the desk over there."

"Drew, I'm comfortable! I don't want to sit on the desk!"

"Ok, then how 'bout the top of the refrigerator?"

"What? Are you joking? That's so unsanitary and gross!"

"No it isn't."

"Yes it is."

"No it isn't. Sweets, you're being very difficult tonight."

"*I'm* being difficult? You're the one who's being difficult. I don't understand where all of these ideas have suddenly come from!"

"They haven't suddenly come from...anywhere."

"Oh really. You just suddenly decided out of the blue that we have to have sex on top of the fridge?"

So, this is what happens when you give away the milk for free, I thought to myself.

There's no rest for the wicked.

Vive La Revenge

Today was the last day of my two-week practicum at Frieda's Finishing School. I was supposed to teach in last period this afternoon, and I spent my entire lunch hour going over my lesson plan and making sure everything was in order. I got to the classroom on time and set myself up at the front. The girls were excited that I was going to be teaching them, and I had just begun the lesson when Shane suddenly appeared and told me to have a seat at the back. I was completely confused, and then saw a girl standing and smiling behind him. She squeezed his hand as they exchanged an amorous glance, then regarded me with a haughty air. She had on a black turtle neck, a long denim skirt and black basketball shoes. She looked like she was in her early twenties. She also looked like she was at least a "double C" cup.

It turned out she was "Nadine," the new French teaching assistant whom Shane had told me nothing about. I watched her from the back of the room where I was sitting with some of the more "lively," (i.e., behaviorally challenged) girls. I was furious. Shane knew that I needed him to evaluate my lesson to meet college requirements, and he also knew how hard I had been working on this lesson plan. It was Friday afternoon, and my last day at the school. I was screwed, chewed, and barbecued.

I knew that some of the girls were watching me to see my reaction to the unexpected turn of events. I looked out the window and tried to calm down, thinking about what to do.

"Miss! Miss!"

Two girls that I'd also been teaching in Eileen's drama class were giggling beside me. I kneeled down next to their desks to ask what they wanted.

"How do you say, 'Shane is dead' in French?"

"Um…"

Shane and Nadine were both looking at me.

"Why would you want to say that?" Shane asked.

I wonder, I muttered under my breath.

I sat back down at my desk and thought about how outrageous the entire situation was. I found it interesting that there were so many young and attractive female "language assistants" in the International Languages department.

The girls were warming up to Nadine, who was told that I was a "French Canadian". Looking at me with disdain, she asked me if I was from that "backward province where you can't understand the French—Quebec?" The classroom erupted in laughter as I sank lower into my chair. I responded quietly in English, *No*. As Nadine answered questions from the girls, I found myself feeling more and more distressed that she had hijacked my lesson, my afternoon, and my teaching evaluation. Then again, Shane was really the one to blame. The tension was beginning to mount between all three of us in the classroom.

OK. Three of us can play this game, I thought.

I decided to put my acting skills to use.

Leaning back in my chair, I looked at Nadine with the same expression that Shane has when he evaluates my lessons: Curiously.

Hmm…What is it that you're trying to say, Mademoiselle Arrogante? I wrinkled my forehead as though concentrating furiously. I noticed her smile wavering as she watched me. Good. My plan was working. I leaned even further back in my chair, right leg extended dramatically over my left and tapped my pen against my desk, thinking,

Hmm…Shall I give you a B plus or a C minus for today's performance? I don't know. I'm not much of a fan of denim skirts.

Then I looked at her once more, making sure I had her gaze, and thought, *C minus it is. Sorry, Amélie.*

And with a flourish, I wrote a big "C minus" on my notepad. Of course, it meant nothing, but she didn't know that.

Nadine suddenly stopped talking mid-sentence and frowned unhappily, turning to Shane for guidance. Shane looked at me with his eyebrows raised and I gave him an icy stare thinking, *You brought this on your own damn self Mr. Why Don't I Just Import a French Coquette and Ruin Lindsay's Teaching Career While I'm At It?*

Realizing that I was the cause of the stalled lesson, thirty-five heads turned around to fix me with a questioning gaze. I was sitting in the back corner with my arms across my chest, glaring defiantly at Shane. *And that, Monsieur, is how I can topple your classroom in two minutes, without speaking a word,* I said to him in French.

He looked momentarily stunned, then regained his composure. "Come see me after class, Mademoiselle Breyer."

Much to the chagrin of George, not to mention Frieda, I ended up with an "A" for my practicum placement.

Chapter Eleven
September - Part II

Trippy Events and Cosmic Disasters

Dear Diary,

I think the world is finally coming to an end. There was a small meteorite crash two nights ago, next door at Edward and Pippa's house. The meteor fell through the roof of their house where there is now a large hole. Luckily, it landed in the living room and everyone was safe inside the kitchen.

Drew and I were away and didn't witness anything, so unfortunately, I have nothing very enlightening to say to the reporters who have been camped outside the house. Edward, Pippa and the kids have gone to Pippa's parents' house in Auckland to escape the media frenzy.

Bryce says that things have been totally "trippy" since he came to Wellington. I'll say. I keep waiting for Ashton Kutcher to show up on the doorstep and tell me that I've been "Punk'd." Except that I'm not famous, so the chances of that are unlikely.

Girl, You've Got it Goin' On

In completely unrelated news, the quality of my sex life has been fluctuating wildly.

Drew's bedroom is right above Bryce and I can't relax. A typical scenario:

"Drew, not now. Bryce can hear us."

"No he can't."

"Yes he can."

"No he can't." (Massaging my back)

"You're so...beautiful. You're so...more-ish."

(I love when he says "more-ish." A Canadian/American guy could never get away with that.)

"Drew...oh...ok. Go get a condom."

"I want to pump you. I want to please you. I want you to feel me loving you."

"Uh huh."

"You're so beautiful and sexy. I love how you feel. I want to put my..."

"Drew! Shhh!"

"...of you! I want you to..."

"Drew!"

"...me! I can't get enough of your..."

"A-hem!" (Bryce coughs and the paper-thin walls make it sound as though he's inches away from us).

"Drew—*stop!*"

By this time, Drew is completely oblivious to the fact that our flat mate is not only listening but embarrassed to death at everything he's saying. I am completely mortified and all I can think about is how I'm going to face Bryce at breakfast the next morning.

While I'm half-listening for Bryce to cough again and trying to make sure the bed doesn't creak, I'm also distracted by other things: *The curtains are in the wash...Are there still reporters outside covering the meteorite crash? Can they see us? Why can't Drew wear something besides white cotton underwear?*

"Why don't you hop up on me?"

Drew's favorite position, not mine. It's too much work.

"It's cold Drew. You stay on top of me."

"I want to look at you. You climb up on me. Please."

"Oh, alright."

...

"Ouch!"

"Sorry."

"Can you be more gentle please?"

Now I just want to climb off and go to sleep. A sudden thought—did he remember to put on the condom?

"Did you remember to put on the condom?"

"Just a second."

Unbelievable. I try not to fall off while he reaches into the drawer of the night table to get a condom. It isn't even a ribbed "For Her Pleasure" condom, but a plain, old standard condom that we got for free from the doctor's office.

I close my eyes and try to concentrate. I can't. I'm too cold and I don't want to make any noise because I know that Bryce is still awake.

I try to concentrate but keep thinking...I should be on the bottom. This is tiring.

Drew doesn't seem to notice.

"I want you to pump me. I want you to..."

"A-hem!"

Bryce clears his throat again.

I am beside myself. I finally give up and do the unthinkable: I fake an orgasm. It's either that, or I stay up half the night trying to concentrate on relaxing while I freeze to death and wonder whether Bryce is going to tell all of our friends about my nocturnal adventures the next day.

The unbelievable has happened: I'm not enjoying sex with Drew, the most gorgeous guy I've ever met. This is how I know that the world has truly come to an end. Plus the fact that meteorites are now crashing through our neighbors' living room ceiling.

Nocturnal Instincts

Another of my newly discovered sexual "hang-ups" relates to Miles. I now refuse to have sex when he stays over on the weekend.

"He's asleep Lindsay! He's in another room. He can't hear anything."

"Well, he could still be listening subconsciously. It isn't good for him."

"He's only three years old. He doesn't understand what's going on."

"Of course he does! He must think I'm in pain!"

"It's natural."

"No, it isn't."

"Yes, it is."

"No, it isn't."

Pause.

"You're very beautiful."

"Oh, OK. Do you have a condom?"

Inevitably, just as I'm about to climax, Miles will wake up.

"Miles is awake!"

Nothing is as unromantic as switching from girlfriend to Step-Mommy Mode.

"Daddy? Lindsay?"

Miles knocks at the door as he calls to us from the other side.

"Lindsay? Can you play Bonny Bobby Shaftoe for me?"

I bought a small keyboard for Miles while I was at Frieda's Finishing School and his favorite song is Bonny Bobby Shaftoe.

"Not now, Sweetheart."

"Mi-iles. Go back to bed."

I don't know why Drew is always telling Miles to go back to bed, because he never does until he gets a cookie or a glass of juice, and all three of us know it.

Drew is always remarkably unruffled as he gets dressed and takes care of his charge. I want to die. How do parents cope with this sort of thing on a regular basis? It's as though Miles has an innate radar, and he knows when something (i.e., an orgasm) is about to happen. Which is when he wakes up and needs a drink, a cookie, or a bedtime lullaby.

"But I *need* Lindsay to play Bonny Bobby Shaftoe."

I'm convinced it's some kind of protective measure to prevent Drew and me from having a baby and introducing a sibling rival.

"He should be sleeping Drew. Get him settled again. I'll make it up to you in the morning."

Bed Bugs and Broom Sticks

Dear Diary,

I have scabies mite. My entire body is itchy. I want to die. I also want to march down to Drew's work and demand that his supervisor, Diane, take responsibility for this latest domestic catastrophe. I finally met her last week at the grocery store where she was walking barefoot in the frozen foods section. Apparently, one of the boys that Drew takes care of on the psychiatric ward, keeps infecting the other patients at the hospital where he works. I have to keep applying, and re-applying, a topical lotion from scalp to toe. It is hell. I feel like a contestant on *Survivor*. Drew, Bryce and I have been meticulously washing all of our clothing and bed sheets every few days, only to discover that we have been infected yet again.

Thankfully, Miles is OK and seems like any other three year old, constantly demanding cookies and wanting to watch The Flintstones, which I forbade because of the negative messages about women. Drew and I do not see eye to eye on this issue, but I am digging my heels in. If Miles is going to be my stepson, I am determined that he will have a healthy respect for women.

I've been letting him help me sweep the floor and do other domestic chores with me, even though Drew doesn't approve. He likes playing with the broom although he always ends up getting the floor even more dirty. One day his future wife will thank me for raising such a liberated man.

Affirmations
I am grounded and comfortable in my body
I do not feel the need to scratch

A Phone Call Away From A Crisis
"Don't phone her back, Drew. I mean it."

"Sweets, she says she needs my help. I won't be a moment."

"No! Give me the phone. We have plans tonight. If you call her, you're just going to end up arguing and we'll never leave."

"We're not going to argue."

Drew and I were standing in the living room where he was holding his car keys in one hand, and the cordless telephone in the other.

"Please! That's what you always say. Let's just go. Come on! Put your A into G!"

"You're so cheeky! Who taught you that?"

"Your Mum. Come on Drew! We have reservations."

"Sweets, I just have to make this call."

"Why are you so stubborn? You don't have to make this call. You *want* to make this call. She's just baiting you. She's going to get on the phone and say, 'Oh, hi dah'lin' and then she'll tell you she's been thinking about filing for a new custody arrangement, and you'll end up on the phone for the rest of the night!"

"Ahem!"

Bryce cleared his throat loudly from his bedroom.

"Sweets, she just needs some help with her taxes."

"Her taxes? Wasn't tax season months ago? You're enabling her!"

"No, I'm not."

"Yes you are."

"No, I'm not."

"Yes you are."

"Lindsay…you look very beautiful tonight."

"Stop trying to flatter me. It's not going to work."

"Ok, Gorgeous. But you still look very beautiful. Is that a new dress?"

"Drew, can we please go? Seriously. I've really been looking forward to having dinner out. You're always getting called to work night shift. I hardly see you. Can we please just leave?"

The door to Bryce's bedroom opened and I heard him go to the bathroom and slam the door shut.

"Dah'lin', just let me make this call and we'll leave right away. I promise."

"I don't believe you. It's going to be exactly like that toaster thing."

"What toaster thing?"

"See! You don't even remember because this happens so often, it's just normal to you. Why do you always have to jump when she calls?"

"I don't jump when she calls. Lindsay, I have to see her for the rest of Miles' life. I've been trying to establish a good relationship with her. You should want a good relationship too. Why don't you try to be friendlier to her on the phone?"

"Oh, there's a good idea. Why don't I just serve some tea and crumpets the next time she drops by to 'confront' me?"

The toilet flushed, and Bryce appeared in the living room wearing his knapsack.

"Have a lovely evening," he said sarcastically before leaving through the back door.

"Lindsay, you're being very cheeky tonight," said Drew.

"Drew, you just aren't being realistic about the situation. She manipulates you and you don't even realize it."

"She doesn't manipulate me."

"OK then, she doesn't. Can we just go?"

"Let me have the phone, Lindsay."

"Fine. I think you and I need to take another break."

"Fine, if that's what you want Sweets," he said absentmindedly.

"Fine."

***

Drew ended up on the phone for two hours and by the time he finished, I had long since changed out of my dress and changed my mind about the strength of our relationship. Nathan was right. He's Mr. Maybe. A big maybe. If I had to choose an ice-cream flavor to describe where things seem to be headed right now, it would be Rocky Road.

Why It Is Never a Good Idea to Have Sex While On 'A Break'

I woke up this morning beside Drew, not wearing any clothes, and when I looked over at him he was fast asleep with what looked like a smirk on his face. I'm beginning to understand why he hasn't seemed overly concerned about our "breaks."

Yesterday, I decided that I wasn't going to spend another evening cooped up in the house alone, so I got a ride from Bryce into town and found an Irish pub. The servers were impressed to meet a Canadian from Toronto and after a couple of vodka coolers, I was feeling much better about myself and life in general.

Then my cell phone rang and it was Drew, asking where I was. I told him I was getting drunk at an Irish pub.

"What! You're doing *what?*"

"I'm getting drunk at an Irish pub," I informed him. "And catching up in fashion—I brought copies of Australian *Vogue* and *Elle Magazine* to read."

"Who are you with?"

He sounded jealous for someone who's supposed to be on a break.

"I'm not with anyone," I told him. "I came by myself."

"There's blokes there. I can hear their voices."

"No one's here but the wait staff."

"Shall I come pick you up? Miles has been asking for you."

Drew knows that I'll always cave and do what if he wants if Miles is involved in any way.

"OK. I'll meet you outside."

"Daddy! Tell her it's a surprise."

"What surprise Drew?"

"Oh, Miles and I have a surprise for you."

"OK. See you soon."

I couldn't imagine what the surprise was.

***

"He's—orange and furry and he bounces all around!"

Miles was very excited when I saw him in the car.

"Shh...Miles. It's a surprise."

"Daddy got Lindsay a surprise! But you *can't* pull his tail!"

Miles was pointing his finger at me, and I laughed until I turned and saw Drew's face. He was still unhappy that I had been out drinking. I banged my head on the roof of the car when I tried to get inside and he muttered something that sounded like "drunk as a skunk".

When we got home, I was introduced to "Tigger Jr.," an alley cat with fleas and a nasty gash on his head, amongst other injuries sustained during a fight with a group of tomcats. Drew says Helena thought he would be the best person to nurse him back to health, but I personally think she's trying to make my life miserable. I've already had enough problems with Tigger Sr. who has destroyed about fifteen pairs of pantyhose since I moved in. Suffice to say, Tigger Jr. wasn't quite the "surprise" I had been expecting. I reached over to pet the top of his head and he promptly sunk his teeth into my hand.

"Ouch! You bloody..."

"Sweets! Don't forget, little ears are listening."

Miles looked up at me with a wide-eyed expression and pointed his finger again.

"Lindsay! Be nice!"

"Sorry, Cutie-pie."

I've decided that Tigger Jr. is going to be Drew's cat, although I can already guess who will end up feeding him.

A Symphony of Ire

"DREW? DROO-OO, where are you?" A loud singsong voice pierced the comfortable silence of the house.

Helena. Damn! She wasn't supposed to be here for another two hours.

"Has he gone out then, Helena? I'm desperate for a drink of something cold." A second voice, raspy and slightly breathless chimed in, adding a wistful note to the loud symphony shattering the tranquillity of my afternoon.

"Shut up, Mother! DREW! DROO-OO!"

Damn! How do I get out of this one?

I was drying my hair in the shower, skin still damp from the warm water that moments earlier had enveloped me in a cocoon of blissful, herbal-scented steam. I had decided to try a new aromatherapy bath gel, which promised to send me into a state of dreamy relaxation. Unfortunately, all the lavender and chamomile in the world couldn't undo the knots in my neck that developed after hearing Helena's voice.

I looked out the window, and felt the sudden impulse to jump. Tigger Jr., as though reading my thoughts, sprang onto the window sill, looked at me with a plaintive meow, then contemplated the ground below, before gracefully leaping down to the grass where he landed with impressive agility.

"Traitor!" I hissed at him. "Thanks for nothing!"

Just then, the door swung open revealing a surprised Helena, who must have decided to use the "loo".

"Lindsay!" She exclaimed, looking none too pleased to see me in my almost-naked state.

"Helena! Hi! I was just finishing my shower."

I untied and retied my towel around the top of my chest, and tried to step casually over the bathtub ledge.

"Who were you talking to?" Helena asked, left eyebrow arched in suspicion.

"Me? Oh—no one. I was just talking to Tigger Jr."

Helena looked around the bathroom, then back at me with both eyebrows raised.

"He's outside in the garden now," I explained.

"I don't see him anywhere."

"Helena! Helena, is that Drew? Oh—Lindsay! How are you dear?"

Yolanda's face peered through the doorway, reading glasses magnifying her huge blue eyes.

"I'm fine, Yolanda. If you ladies will excuse me for a second, I'll throw on some jeans and be right back down." I slipped past the two matriarchs, hoping to buy myself a few minutes of personal time before I had to face the proverbial music.

"Lindsay! Isn't *your* room down the hall?" Helena asked pointedly, as I started towards the stairs to Drew's bedroom.

"Yes! Yes it is. What am I thinking?" I laughed, hoping I sounded light and breezy.

I turned back and headed into "my" room, which had been converted into a playroom for Miles. The floor was littered with train set pieces, marbles, stuffed toys, and a keyboard. There were of course, no clothes in the now-empty wardrobe that Drew had eventually managed to bring inside from the garage.

What do I do now?

I stood by the door, opening it a crack, and poked my head out.

I could see Helena and Yolanda in the kitchen, where Helena was opening and closing the cupboard doors, apparently trying to find a clean glass to get Yolanda something to drink. Yolanda had settled in at the kitchen table and had taken out a ball of yarn and a pair of crochet needles. *Wonderful.*

Drew was still at the hospital and wouldn't be home until his shift ended, an hour from now. I had no idea where Bryce was—probably playing snooker at the pub.

Bryce! That gave me an idea.

Poking my head out the door again, I waited until Helena's back was turned, and Yolanda's head was down, then quickly slipped out the doorway and into Bryce's bedroom.

Words cannot describe the disgusting mess that I found there. The bed was unmade and the sheets looked like they hadn't been washed in months, which was probably a fair assumption. There was a pizza box opened on the floor, with two congealed slices exposed to the air. Dirty socks and underwear were thrown haphazardly around the floor, and were probably to blame for the horrible stench that filled the room. A large Ché poster hung on the wall, and a small stereo with a cluttered pile of CDs stood on Bryce's desk, which didn't look as though it got used very often—at least, not for schoolwork.

I walked over to the window and opened it, taking deep breaths of fresh air.

Then I turned to Bryce's dresser, which was covered in a pile of condoms, empty cigarette packets, matches, two baseball caps and an unopened bottle of Aqua Velva.

Lovely.

I opened the middle drawer, hoping to find a small T-shirt. Instead, I found myself face-to-face with what seemed to be an extensive stash of porn. There were magazines, DVDs and what looked like something inflatable in a cardboard box.

Gross! I quickly slammed the drawer shut, and tried the next one.

Two minutes later, I had finally found a reasonably clean T-shirt and a faded pair of black track pants. Both were about five sizes too big for me.

I let my towel drop to the floor, preparing to pull the T-shirt over my head.

"Lindsay!"

"Get out!" I yelled, trying to cover myself with the T-shirt.

The bedroom door, which had unexpectedly swung open, now quickly slammed shut. I don't think I've ever seen such an expression on Bryce's face before: it was a mixture of confusion, surprise and delight.

"Is everything alright?" Helena's voice boomed from the kitchen.

"It's fine!" Bryce and I called back in unison. I was pulling on Bryce's clothes as fast as I could.

There was a hesitant knock at the door, and I decided that despite my extreme embarrassment, Bryce might prove to be a useful ally.

"Come in."

Bryce, cheeks flushed, looked at me with a saucy grin and cleared his throat.

"Sorry to disturb. Did you find what you were looking for?"

"Bryce! This isn't funny. I need your help."

"What?"

"I want you to go upstairs and get me something to wear. Make sure Helena doesn't see you!"

"You want me to get you something from Drew's room?" he asked, raising his voice.

"Shhh! It's *our* room, but—whatever. Yes! Please hurry!"

"Perhaps we could work out an arrangement. One good turn deserves another, eh?"

"Bryce, you just saw me naked! That should buy me enough favors for the rest of the year. Now go! Go!" I pushed him away from the door and watched him slowly head up the stairs towards Drew's bedroom.

I pulled the door in and sat back down on Bryce's bed. Not long afterwards, I watched a blue rucksack fall from the sky and into Drew's prized rhododendrons. I went to the window and pushed it open, just in time to see Bryce shimmying down the drainpipe on the side of the house.

"What are you doing?" I asked, not without a hint of panic.

"You aren't leaving me here alone with them are you?"

"Sorry, Your Majesty. Got a date with Sydney tonight. Can you pass us a couple of condoms?"

I shook my head in disgust, and grabbed a couple of condom packages from the dresser.

"Here. Thanks for nothing!"

"Ta. Here's your clothes. Have a lovely visit," he grinned, before sprinting around the side of the house, and out of sight.

Well, I sighed to myself. *I guess things can't get worse.*

***

"Mum! What do you mean you won't pay for the wedding? Bloody hell, how do you expect us to get married then?"

Drew's face was red, and I squirmed in my seat as the couple sitting across from us looked over with an amused expression.

Drew, Helena, Yolanda, Miles and I were all sitting by the bay window of a Thai restaurant where Drew had insisted we come for dinner. Helena preferred Italian, and Yolanda was in the mood for fish and chips, but Drew insisted on Thai, so Thai it was. Yolanda had sulked for a good fifteen minutes in front of her menu, declaring there was nothing edible on it, before Helena finally told her to "shut up" and made a special request to the kitchen for the closest thing to English cuisine.

Now, Yolanda was toying unhappily with her crispy filet fish, while Miles played with his pan-fried jelly noodles, oblivious to the storm brewing around him.

Drew, Helena and I had all chosen the Chef's Special: Pa-Nang Curry Seafood, which I had already managed to spill down the front of my bleach-stained T-shirt. Bryce had done me no favours when he chose an outfit for me to wear: the only things I found in the blue rucksack were the old T-shirt I was wearing, distinguished by yellow deodorant stains under the arms, my white cashmere skirt and a pair of Reef denim flip flops. When Drew came home and asked whether I wanted to change, I shot him a dark look and told him I was perfectly comfortable the way I was, while Helena looked at us warily. Now, as I had feared, our celebratory dinner was turning into a Christianson family holy war, that didn't show signs of abating.

"Drew, I will not keep doling out money for your every passing fancy!"

I was a bit taken aback by this remark, and avoided Yolanda's sympathetic gaze as I stared down at my red curried seafood.

"Lindsay is not a passing fancy! She's going to be my wife!"

"And that's what you said about Janine! I spent a fortune on that wedding and now I'll be paying for the next fifteen years! You should never have agreed to that ridiculous settlement!"

"I agreed to do what's best for Miles!" Drew bellowed. "Some of us think of others before ourselves!"

"Oh, and it's easy to think of others when someone else is paying, isn't it?" Helena snapped, her voice burning with ire.

"How much was that engagement ring? That must have cost a pretty penny!"

Four heads turned to look at the offending diamond, which sparkled shamelessly on my wedding ring finger.

I nervously took a bite of shrimp, then gasped as the large crustacean stuck in my throat.

Coughing painfully, I reached my hands to my neck, gasping for air.

"Bloody hell, not again!"

Drew quickly got up from his seat, and ran behind me to administer a well-placed thump on my back.

The shrimp dislodged, and I sat back in my chair, cheeks ablaze and eyes watering.

"Lindsay dear, have some water," Yolanda murmured, pushing her glass towards me.

"Thanks!" I croaked.

"Oh Lindsay," said Helena, looking guilty. "This isn't your fault. Drew has just got to learn some responsibility."

"Mum..."

"No! No more arguing! This is supposed to be a nice meal. Now, I'd like to propose a toast."

Miles perked up when he heard this, and we all turned to look at Helena, who had raised her wine glass in the air.

"To Drew and Lindsay. May you both bring each other great happiness."

"Lindsay! Lindsay! Lindsay!" yelled Miles, banging his fork on the table.

"Those manners! It's absolutely shocking. Drew, is this what you teach the boy at home?" asked Yolanda, as her youngest grandson glared at her.

"Mother..." Helena started to say.

"Do shut up!" yelled Miles, gleefully.

Yolanda turned pink with indignation, and the rest of us hid our smiles behind our napkins, grateful the storm had passed.

I told myself that as far as future in-laws go, I could have done worse. Well, I also could have done better, but for tonight, I was making the conscious decision to see my wine glass as half-full, instead of half-empty.

Affirmations
I am a brave, confident, capable woman
I believe in miracles, and I now welcome their manifesting
Each and every moment of my life,
Brings new possibilities...

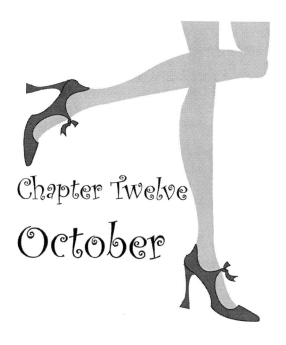

Chapter Twelve
October

Everything I Didn't Want to Know About My Ex-Boyfriend's Engagement

Dear Diary,

As though my day wasn't already going badly enough (had an argument with Drew this morning; hair frizzier than usual; no clean underwear in the drawer), I received a package this afternoon from Nathan.

Dear Lindsay,

How's life in New Zealand? Eating lots of kiwis? Hope that psycho chic (forget her name) isn't still bugging you.

Heads up on the pink envelope attached. It's an invitation to Ben's wedding. I didn't know whether to send it or not, but you did date the guy for four years. Figured you'd be bummed after getting this, so I sent a couple of US Magazines.

Take care,

Nathan

P.S. Did you get a chance to look into that wrongful dismissal thing for me? Got the alarm clock you sent for my birthday. You forgot we use different voltage at home.

Thanks anyway.

I hesitated about half a second before tearing open the pink envelope which had my name and address written in gold ink. A gold embossed wedding invitation was inside, along with a handwritten note:

Dear Lindsay,

I came across your name when I was going through our address books to make the guest list for our wedding. Ben has always spoken very highly of you, and I want you to know that because of the wonderful person you are, I now have the amazing fiancé that I do today. Ben tells me that he learned a lot about relationships from you: how to be romantic, how to be patient, how to compromise and share. And so, I've been able to benefit from that and have the incredible romance I do today.

This past year has been like a dream, and we're both so looking forward to starting a new life together. You are always welcome to come visit us when you're in Vancouver. We have a guest bedroom next to the nursery where you can stay. Please feel free to come and see our new house anytime.

Ben and I would be absolutely delighted to have you come to our wedding, and witness our vows as we begin our new journey together as husband and wife. I hope you can make it and look forward to meeting you in person.

Warmest wishes from Ben's ecstatic fiancée,

Marie

Attached to the card was a photograph of Ben with a busty blonde woman, head tilted to the side as she gazed up at him adoringly. They looked like the perfect, happy couple. I wanted to kill them.

Eyes blurring with tears, I grabbed my jacket and raced down the stairs, nearly knocking over Bryce who was wearing nothing but a fuzzy lime-green towel wrapped around his waist.

"All done in the loo. Just going for a lie-down, if you'd like to join me."

"I *wouldn't!*"

"I'm just having a bit of fun, eh?"

"Bryce—just…"

I couldn't finish my sentence, and Bryce's expression changed from one of surprise to one of concern as he watched me brush the angry tears from my face.

"What happened?"

"My ex-boyfriend's fiancée sent me a wedding invitation. Here." I thrust the pink envelope into his hands.

He took a few moments to glance over the wedding invitation and note, then handed them back to me.

"She sounds like a real bitch, eh?"

I managed to smile through my tears, and realized I was glad that Bryce was there to talk to.

"Apparently I'm a training ground for husbands." I took a shaky breath and exhaled.

"Whew! I'm going to the store to get some ice cream and vodka coolers."

"You feel like a drink?"

"Yeah. I think I deserve one."

"Have you still not tried a Speights yet?"

"No."

"We'll go to the pub."

"Oh, Bryce..."

"Half an hour for a pint—like a real Kiwi. Just give me a minute."

I watched as he disappeared into the bedroom, and heard him opening and closing his drawers with a bang. I wondered whether it was a good idea to go to the pub with him, but I didn't want to be alone, and Drew was out for the evening.

One pint couldn't hurt...

Why We Always Put Off 'Til Tomorrow What We Should Do Today

Dear Diary,

I'm procrastinating. Really procrastinating. As in, "You know you're procrastinating when..."

Two minutes ago, I actually started typing Google search terms like "quantum physics applications to physical reality" onto the computer screen. Yes, I am desperately trying to avoid what I'm supposed to be doing, which is my psychology assignment due tomorrow morning at 9 am. It is now 6:18 pm and for the past ten hours, I have:

Cooked breakfast for Miles, which consisted of pancakes and table syrup, not real maple syrup, which I can't seem to find despite spending many frustrating hours wandering the aisles at various grocery stores across the city;

Dressed Miles for nursery school, which was a superhuman feat this morning because he did not want to be interrupted while watching Barney the Dinosaur, and kept admonishing me to "Be nice!"

Jogged outside, and got lost, and then finally found the house again after running up and down the same main street wondering which side-road to take while an elderly woman wearing a colourful poncho stared at me;

Done my laundry, and Drew's laundry, and Miles' laundry, and hung the clothes on the line outside with multicoloured plastic pegs, making artful patterns of green, pink and blue while singing the American national anthem (just to provoke my Kiwi neighbours);

Spent time at the expensive High Street Grocers, ostensibly to pick up some tea. I ended up frittering away an hour as I helped myself to free coffee and lemon wafers, and spent $50 on things I hadn't realized I needed (like mozzarella cheese, sliced mangoes, seafood salad, pickles and cranberry juice);

Fought with Bryce over the TV, and threatened to never again assist him with library research if he does not smarten up and start learning to share our limited household resources (he still seems disappointed that nothing "happened" during our evening at the pub, aside from my drinking too much and falling asleep at our booth);

Folded laundry while watching an Oprah Winfrey DVD that Nathan sent me, and cried my eyes out while women revealed their heartbreaking stories of love, loss and betrayal;

Took phone calls from Janine who keeps demanding to know "where my bloody ex-husband is" so that she can confront him with "her truth" and "make him pay" for the consequences of her decision...whatever that means;

Assured Janine that I do not require her hair cutting services, and that there's really no need to drive me straight back to America as I'll probably just fly back, at the end of the year, on my own accord;

Argued with Drew, and insisted that he start answering the phone and taking Janine's calls because I do not appreciate being caught in the middle of this Kiwi version of *War of the Roses*, and,

Washed and conditioned my hair, exfoliated, shaved and moisturized my legs, plucked my eyebrows, waxed my upper lip, and ignored Bryce's rude comments and remarks as I dashed from the bathroom to the bedroom in my housecoat.

In short, I have been doing everything that I normally procrastinate and don't do. The only thing left now is my psychology assignment. One, two, three! I'm still here. OK, I'll just check my email and then I'll really start.

***

Dear Diary,

My life is a complete and utter fiasco. I cannot believe this. I just opened my inbox, and what did I find, but an email from my ex, Ben. The one I warned never to contact me again. The one whose fiancée took the liberty of inviting me to their wedding, sounding for all the world like the cat who just ate the canary and finished the cream bowl. Except that she isn't his fiancée anymore:

Hi Sunshine,

How are you? I know you told me not to call again, so I decided to write.

I found out a couple of weeks ago that Marie sent you a wedding invitation and photo—she shouldn't have done that. I knew you'd be upset but at the time I figured the damage had been done, so I didn't try to contact you to apologize. Hope there weren't too many containers of Haagen Daaz sacrificed for that (smile).

Nathan and I ran into each other at the mall last week. He told me you're getting married to some Kiwi guy. That was fast.

Well, I thought you should know that the wedding is off. It turns out that Marie has been lying to me. Not only is this not her first engagement, but she was actually married to a guy who lives in Ohio. He's a pilot as well—guess she has a thing for that. I asked her how long she thought she could keep hiding this from me. She said she was going to find a way to break the news after the wedding. Not anymore.

You know Lindz, the closer it got to the wedding, the more I realized she's not as perfect as I thought she was. I mean, emotionally. Physically, she's got a beautiful face and a shit-hot body, but emotionally, I don't think she's all there.

You know, I've never met another girl like you, Lindsay. You're smart, and funny, and I keep thinking about the four years we spent together...

Please don't marry this Kiwi guy. You hardly know him. Give us another chance.

Love,

Ben

Dear Ben,

How can you do this to me? Who do you think you are, emailing me after almost a year with this pathetic sob story about your pathetic fiancée who can't stop licking the canary feathers from her lips? If you think I'm coming back to you now, after I've finally got my own life on track and where I want to be, you're wrong.

I AM getting married to this "Kiwi guy". His name's Drew by the way, and he's smarter, and better looking and richer than you (not that money matters, because I'm not as shallow as some people, Mr. Engaged to the Blonde With the "Shit-Hot" Body).

You have no right to try to screw up my life just because yours is going off the rails now. I've been happy. I have a life here. I can finally cross the street without nearly losing my life because I'm checking for traffic in the wrong direction. I know what words like "bun-fight" and "capsicum" mean. I'm staying, and I'm marrying Drew and we're going to be madly, fabulously, happy.

DO NOT email me again. I mean it.

Lindsay

Dear Lindsay,

I love you. Marry me.

Ben

Dear Ben,

I love you? Marry me? That's the way you propose—over email?? In case you didn't understand me the first time, I'm *engaged.* I am not going to come running back to you just because it turns out that Goldilocks is a psychopathic liar. I thought you were in love, and she's amazing and dazzling you with her Masters in English and her fake boobs.

This is your problem, not mine. You need to grow up.

Lindsay

Dear Lindsay,

What can I do to convince you to marry me? Do you want a ring? I can send one by FedEx tomorrow. Will that prove that I love you?

Ben

P.S. They aren't fake.

Dear Ben,

Thank you for the romantic gesture, but I already have a ring and I didn't get it from FedEx. What's wrong with you? Why can't you take "no" for an answer?

Lindsay

Dear Lindsay,

Because I love you and I realized that I've never stopped loving you. You're the woman I want to spend the rest of my life with.

Just think about it. That's all I'm asking.

Think about it.

Ben

Betwixt and Between

"I want to kill him."

"Mmmm…"

"I mean *really* kill him."

"Mmmm…"

"Sydney, are you listening to me?"

"What? Sorry, Lindsay. I'm just thinking about what to wear to the pub tonight."

"Girl's night out?"

"Mmm. I met a very yummy bloke last week. He's supposed to be at The Pump with his mates to play pool."

"Who's all going?"

"Just my sister and a couple of friends."

"Why didn't you invite me?"

"Are you serious? You haven't been out on a Friday night with me ever since you got engaged. It's just been bridal magazines, and baking for Miles, and arguments with Drew, and what shall the bridesmaids wear…"

"Sydney! I'm getting married! What do you expect?"

"So you are getting married then? You're not calling it off and going back to—what's his name? Glen?"

"Ben."

"You're not going back to Ben?"

"I don't know what I'm doing. That's why I'm asking for your advice. Who do you think I should choose?"

"How should I know? I haven't slept with either of them."

"Sydney, be serious."

"I am. Who's better in bed? There's your answer."

"I don't know who's better. They're different."

"Different good, or different bad?"

"Just different. It's fine with both of them."

"Jesus, you're thinking of getting married to someone who's just 'fine'? I'd rather poke my eyes out with a sharp object."

I watched as she took a long drag on her cigarette.

"Sydney, not all of us are sex addicts."

"Are you calling me a sex addict?" Her luminous green eyes were now flashing with anger.

"You know what I mean."

"Lindsay," Sydney took one last drag on her cigarette, then dropped it on the floor, and ground it out with a well-practiced stiletto heel.

"Just because I like sex, does not make me a sex addict. You know, you think you're open-minded because you do yoga and meditate, and all this other Hollywood crap, but the truth is, you're judgmental."

"I'm not..."

"Hang on a bit, I'm not finished. You've never said it, but you look down on me for sleeping with blokes and not getting emotionally attached. You think it's wrong to have sex for fun because everyone should be like you, getting their kickers in a knot when they're not engaged by twenty-nine."

"Sydney, I don't..."

"For the past nine months, I've listened to you go on about every silly cow who's ever shown you her diamond ring. Who the fuck cares? If someone's life is so miserable that she needs to show you her jewellery to feel better, you should feel sorry for her. But you don't. It just makes you feel miserable about your own life and fixate on everything you don't have. You know what really rankles you Lindsay? It was never the diamond ring. It's the fact that those women thought they were better than you. Just like you think you're better than me."

Sydney stood up and slung her handbag over her shoulder.

"If you really want my advice as a friend, then make your decision based on what you think will bring you more happiness, not what you think will make you happy."

There was a long pause as we both looked at each other.

"Sydney," I ventured, trying to think of something to say to bridge the sudden gap between us.

"Please don't think I look down on you. I don't. You're the most beautiful and vibrant person I know. I admire you. Honestly. I'm just going through a personal crisis, and I'm disappointed that you don't seem to be there for me."

"Lindsay, do you think being proposed to by two men when all you've wanted is to get married, is a crisis?"

I was silent.

"I'll tell you what a personal crisis is. That was my last cigarette. *That*, is a personal crisis."

And with that, Sydney turned on her pointed stiletto heel, and swept out of the cafeteria, leaving me utterly confused. *What was she talking about?*

One of "Those" Girls
Or,
Sex is Like Pizza

I can't sleep. I keep thinking about the decision I have to make: Staying in New Zealand and marrying Drew, or going home to marry Ben. How do I decide? It feels as though whatever decision I make, I'll be left wondering whether it was the right one. I've come to a crossroads, and the only thing I know for sure, is there's no going back.

As I was trying to fall asleep, I remembered the angst-filled time that my girlfriend Sophie went through when she got married, five years ago. Sophie was in the unfortunate position of being from the wrong religion, according to her fiancé's family, who are Jewish. They had high hopes for their son Zack to marry a doe-eyed, curly-haired girl from a "good" Jewish family, and they didn't try to hide their disapproval.

Far from the Jewish ideal, Sophie comes from a French-Dutch

background, with wheat-colored hair, cerulean eyes, and milk-white skin. She may as well have had the word "Aryan" tattooed across her forehead. Sophie had always complained of Zack being a "Mama's boy," who wouldn't stand up to his family. Shortly after proposing to her, he confessed that the news had sent his mother, Shoshanna, into a mental state requiring Valium. Shoshanna accused him of "killing her," and wondered what horrible fate had befallen the family, for her only son to break her heart by marrying a Catholic "shiksa." She claimed the humiliation was so great, she could no longer meet her friends for bridge at the country club, and was now considered an object of pity by the Jewish community.

During the engagement, Zack came down with the flu, and Shoshanna was instantly by his side. She wasted no time in packing her floral suitcases, making an enormous pot of matzah ball soup, and moving into his tiny condominium. As a registered naturopath with her own practice, there was no doubt in her mind that she was the only one qualified to take care of her son. Sophie, meanwhile, was furious. As a nurse, she was equally confident that she was the best person to take care of Zack as he recovered. Zack, for his part, seemed to enjoy all of the attention and made little effort to quell the rising tension between the two women.

Shoshanna went so far as to tell Sophie that she and Zack's father were still confident of persuading Zack to consider dating a "nice Jewish doctor" they knew from the community. Still, despite Shoshanna's best efforts to drive a wedge between the couple, the engagement continued, and I was invited to the bridal shower thrown by Sophie's sister. At the time, I was "seeing" someone that I wasn't sure I liked, and considered myself to be very single.

The shower did not turn out to be the light-hearted affair I had hoped for. After eating lunch, which consisted of matzah ball soup, fresh fruit and pastries, Sophie's sister had us play a game that she assured everyone would be a "total riot". Sitting in a small circle, all of the girls took turns answering questions that Sophie's sister had prepared and emailed to our significant others. Our job was to guess which answer our significant others had selected. The winner was the one who correctly guessed the most answers chosen by their significant other.

It was a complete and utter fiasco.

They say that women are far more competitive with each other than men. This is especially true when it comes to comparing each other's relationships. I had never seen so many crestfallen and visibly angered women in one room. The topics covered ranged from personal intrusions such as questions about sex, to how annoying the woman in question could be.

Example #1

I consider her lovemaking skills to be:
 a) Awesome! She's a hot, passionate lover.
 b) Not bad—they could use some work.
 c) Sex is like pizza—even when it's bad, it's good.
 d) Brutal. If things don't improve, I'm out of here.

Example #2

When she talks to me, I think:
 a) God, I wish she would just shut up.
 b) I wonder what's on TV right now?
 c) She's so cute.
 d) This is my soul mate.

Example #3

The name of the book my Sweetie is currently reading is:
(Fill in the blank)

One the whole, the men who answered the questions gave painfully honest answers. It was a rude awakening for many of us sitting around our "circle of truth" (or eighth circle of hell, depending on who you were). After one girl, who had been married the longest, was awarded the lowest score, she burst into tears and abruptly left the party which put an even wetter blanket on the festivities. Sophie had a strained smile on her face, having placed second last, and I was furiously seething inside, having discovered that my soon to be ex had revealed his secret wish that I would just "shut-up".

The only person in the room who didn't look like she wanted to grab her cell phone and immediately file for divorce was Luanne, another friend from university. Luanne had recently married, and strangely, her score was ten points higher than the second-highest score, attained by

Sophie's long and happily married cousin, Anne-Lise. Luanne smiled triumphantly as she accepted her prize, a gift bag from The Body Shop filled with scented candles, bath gel, and other goodies I'm sure the rest of us felt we were more deserving of, since apparently we were all dating complete and total losers.

I couldn't help but think that Luanne and her husband had been in cahoots and cheated. The significant others had all been emailed the questions with the proviso that they were not to show them to the women in their lives or it would spoil the game. So, Luanne, either a) has a husband who can supernaturally read her mind, or b) has a husband who might not be able to read her mind, but loves and respects her enough to help her cheat and win a bridal shower game. Either way, Luanne had won; the proud tilt of her chin and vain glint in her cool, aquamarine eyes, made this abundantly clear.

So, I thought to myself. It's all fun and games until someone (or in this case, almost everyone) realizes their significant other is a jerk. I realized I was the only unmarried woman in the room, aside from Sophie's sister who has been in a six-year relationship with her live-in boyfriend, and has no plans to marry. I wondered whether she was secretly jealous of Sophie and had devised a game sure to shatter her sister's anticipated wedding bliss.

As I was pondering the irony of this, Sophie's mother suddenly broke the depressed silence by loudly inquiring,

"Lindsay, why aren't *you* married?"

Twelve heads quickly turned to look at me, as I prayed for divine intervention. I had no idea what to say, and did not welcome the question or the sudden interest in my personal life. I silently cursed Sophie's mother for attempting to draw attention away from her daughter's unhappiness by using me as a convenient distraction.

"Well, you know…it's hard to say. I mean, I've been busy traveling, and I've been in school for the past four years. I just got accepted to law school in Vancouver…"

I paused, waiting for her to say "congratulations," but she continued staring at me, as though I was speaking a foreign language. Apparently, acceptance to law school is not quite on par with legally committing yourself to a lifetime of self-imposed monogamy.

"I don't know. I guess I haven't met the right person yet."

"Well, I suppose you still have time," she said doubtfully.

I could feel the weight of twelve pairs of eyes on me, and felt my cheeks burn as I imagined their pity.

I promised myself then and there, that as soon as I got home and broke up with Mr. Wrong, I was going to make the best effort I could to find Mr. Right, and throw my own uncomfortable wedding shower, complete with over-protective mother and overbearing future mother-in-law. I was never going to be that girl, the one everyone pitied, again.

O Brother, Where Art Thou?
Dear Nathan,

My life has turned into some kind of badly written soap opera. I can't believe that in less than a year, I've gone from being single with no options, to engaged with one too many.

Who do I choose? Ben was the one, true love of my life, but I don't know whether I want to go back to him after he got engaged to someone else. And so much time has passed...I'm not sure I'm the same person I was when we were together.

Then, there's Drew. He's promising me a healthy inheritance from his Mum, and annual vacations to their hotel property in the Fiji islands. He's good-looking and smart and I'm really attracted to him, but he can also be selfish and lazy. And I'm having a hard time stomaching the thought of Janine, a.k.a. The Best Thing That Ever Happened, being in our lives forever. Miles is adorable, but I could do without Drew's "excess baggage".

Help.

Lindsay

Dear Lindsay,
Why do you ask me these questions? I'm a guy. How should I know?
Nathan

Dear Nathan,

What do you mean, *you're a guy, how should you know?*

You're my brother. You're supposed to help me. Don't forget, whichever guy I choose is going to be your brother-in-law. Don't you have a preference?

Lindsay

Dear Lindsay,
Not really.
Nathan.

Dear Nathan,
Just tell me what you would do if you were in my situation.
Lindsay

Dear Lindsay,
I wouldn't marry either of them.
Nathan

Dear Nathan,
Not an option. Help me choose: Former love of my life who's been engaged and sleeping with someone else (wow—I didn't need that visual), or the handsome, irresponsible (future) millionaire with the nutty ex-wife.
Lindsay

Dear Lindsay,
If you really can't decide, why don't you just flip a coin?
Nathan

Dear Nathan,
I can't flip a coin! This is my life we're talking about, not choosing between chocolate or vanilla at Baskin Robbins. I need your insight. Which one—former love of my life or irresponsible millionaire?
Lindsay

Dear Lindsay,
If you like them both the same, then why don't you just choose the rich guy?
Nathan

Dear Nathan,
So you think I should just put up with his crazy ex-wife for the rest of my life?

Lindsay

Dear Lindsay,
Fine. Then choose the pilot. I could use the free travel passes.
Nathan

Dear Nathan,
What kind of answer is that??
Lindsay

Dear Lindsay,
I told you I don't want to get involved in this. You should just make your own decision.
Nathan

Dear Nathan,
I told you, I can't make a decision, that's why I'm asking for your advice. You're a guy. You're supposed to give me the guy-analysis, like that column in *Cosmo* magazine.
Lindsay

Dear Lindsay,
Why don't you just ask the guy at Cosmo then?
Nathan

Dear Nathan,
Well, since my own brother can't give me more than a two-sentence response (are you playing on-line video games?) I guess I have to.
Lindsay

Dear Lindsay,
Why are you even asking my advice if you're just going to be bitter?
Nathan

Dear Nathan,
I am not bitter.
Lindsay

Dear Lindsay,
Yes you are.
Nathan

Dear Nathan,
No I'm not.
Lindsay.

Dear Lindsay,
Are too.
Nathan.

Dear Nathan,
Am not.
Lindsay

Nathan,
Don't you even miss me?
Lindsay

Lindsay,
You know I do. You just have to give yourself time to make your own
decision. You don't give yourself enough credit. I gotta get some sleep—have an
interview tomorrow morning.
Nathan

Dear Nathan,
OK. Good luck with the interview. What's it for?
Lindsay

Dear Lindsay,
Computer data analyst with Microsoft. Don't worry Lindz, you'll make the
right decision. I know you—you always do.
Nathan

***

Well, I didn't exactly take Nathan's last piece of advice. I emailed
the Cosmo Guy, and then checked my "Yahoo" account every day for the
next week. He finally responded on Friday:

Dear "Indecisive,"
Sounds like they're equally bad choices. If you're that desperate to get married,
why don't you flip a coin?
Cosmo Guy

What the *heck?* Is no one willing to give me advice? I don't get it.

This calls for some extra-strength affirmations:
I am a strong, confident, powerful woman,
Who makes difficult decisions with ease
I am a hot, sexy, genius
I am a hot, sexy, genius who,
Makes difficult decisions with ease

***

Dear Diary,

I've been thinking about Sydney's outburst in the cafeteria. After she left, I felt more confused than anything else because I've never seen her that angry. But now I wonder whether she has a point. Maybe I am judgmental. I've always thought there must be something wrong with women who say they don't want to get married or have children; that they're fooling themselves. But maybe Sydney really is happy with her life the way it is.

I've also been thinking about the last thing she said to me, "make your decision based on what you think will bring you more happiness, not what you think will make you happy."

Getting married is what will make me happy. Damn. Is that her point?

***

Drew walked in on me this afternoon while I was meditating/positively affirming myself.

"So you're a hot, sexy genius, eh? Why don't you hop into bed with me? I'll show you something hot and sexy."

"Drew! Why can't you knock?"

"We're engaged, Sweets! I don't have to knock."

"Yes you do! I still need privacy."

"We're getting married. You don't have privacy when you're married."

"You don't?"

"Not much."

"But—that doesn't sound right. Who told you that?"

"I was married for three years."

"Well, our marriage doesn't have to be the same as yours and Janine's. Look how that turned out."

"Oh…Sweets. I forgot to tell you. She's off on vacation next week. I've got my practicum to do. You don't mind looking after Miles do you?"

"*What?* I have my finals next week!"

"Shivers! I reckon you'll have to give them a miss, eh?"

"Give them *a miss?* Are you joking? They're my finals, Drew! There's no way I'm missing them! Do you want me to fail my year?"

"Sweets, I need to finish my practicum, or I won't graduate, eh?"

"And I need to write my finals or *I* won't graduate! My parents paid $20,000 to send me here!"

"Mum can pay them back."

"Drew—are you *crazy?* There's no *way* I'm missing my finals! I've worked my *butt* off this year. I want my degree!"

"Please don't yell, Sweets. Miles can hear you. You'll just have to ask administration to defer your exams 'til next semester. They make allowances for family emergencies."

"But this isn't an emergency! This is your ex-wife being totally irresponsible with *your* child."

"Sweets, you're…"

"No! No Drew! This is *your* responsibility! I'm not having it!"

"Sweets…"

"No! Miles can go to your mother's, or her mother's, I don't care. I am *not* sacrificing my school year!"

"Sweets, you're getting very upset. Why don't we hop into bed together, eh? We'll talk about it tomorrow."

"Drew—no. The answer is no."

"Fine then. Let's have a cuddle. I haven't seen you in that new lingerie I bought. You're looking very beautiful tonight."

"Drew…I mean 'no.' I can't do this anymore."

"Do what?"

"I can't."

"Sweets, you're very tired. I think you should get some sleep. You'll feel better in the morning."

"Drew, I don't think you're hearing me right now. I can't do this."

"Lindsay, what are you saying?"

"I just…I'm sorry. I can't do this anymore."

"Look, if it's about Janine, we can hire someone eh? Mum's in Brisbane next week, Janine's parents are—not sure what they're doing, but we'll find someone to look after Miles."

"No Drew, you're not listening. It's not about next week, it's not about Janine. It's everything. It's Janine, the living situation, Miles…I can't live like this. I just can't."

"Sweets…"

"Please don't. Please. You—are great. You're good looking, and smart and I know all those things, but I can't…"

"Lindsay, please. Let's get some sleep. You're just tired."

"Drew, I'm sorry."

"Sweets—don't. We'll talk about this in the morning."

"Drew…"

"We'll talk in the morning."

"Nothing's going to change in the morning."

A long silence.

"Is it that bloke in Canada?"

Another long silence.

"So that's it? You don't want to marry me anymore? You're going back to your ex?"

"I'm sorry. I'm so sorry, Drew. Please forgive me."

"Lindsay, don't do this. We've been through heaps together. We're a family now. I know I haven't been as responsible as I should be, but I can change. I promise. Just tell me what you want me to do, and I'll do it."

"Drew, it's too late! You should have been making changes in your life a long time ago for you and for Miles, not for me!"

"Lindsay, please don't do this. You just need some time. Look, we don't have to get married right away. We can just enjoy being engaged and…I'll take you to our family property in Fiji after the semester ends.

It's beautiful, you'll love it there. Just give things some time. You'll change your mind. I know you will."

"No Drew, I won't."

"Lindsay! How can you give up on us so easily? What about Miles?"

"I think it's time for you to start taking some real responsibility for Miles, and time for me to let you and Janine be the parents I know you can be."

"You can't just abandon him! He loves you!"

"That's because I love him too. I think I love him so much, I was willing to sacrifice my own happiness to be a permanent part of his life. But you and Janine are his real parents, Drew, not me."

"Jesus."

"Drew, I'm not going to suddenly disappear. I'll make sure he's prepared before I go, and I'll stay in touch, I promise."

Drew's eyes filled with tears and I felt the corners of my heart tear.

" I hope I'll always be a part of his life, and yours. You're an awesome guy. You just need some time to get yourself together."

"I don't want to break up, Lindsay."

"I know. But I have to."

Chapter Thirteen
November

Oh, Baby!

This evening, Drew and I invited Sydney to play poker at the house. Bryce joined as well, which was unusual since the four of us have never socialized together. Drew began the evening in a cheerful mood, having finished his practicum with flying colors. He was happy to play host, and I was happy to know that we could still spend time altogether without any underlying tension or hostility, given that we were no longer a couple.

"Sydney, can I get you a beer?" Drew asked, while Bryce prepared to deal the next round of cards.

"Just some water, ta. I can't have any alcohol."

"Personal detox?" Drew smiled affably at everyone, enjoying the effects of his third drink of the evening.

"No. I'm pregnant."

There was a moment of stunned silence as Drew and I looked at each other, then at Sydney, and finally at Bryce, who was grinning sheepishly.

"That's...uh...shivers! It's getting cold, eh? Think I'll put a jumper on. Back in a tick."

Drew hastily got up from his chair and disappeared up the stairs.

Sydney was looking at me expectantly, as I tried to figure out whether she was happy or less than ecstatic about her pregnancy.

"Congratulations. Is, um…" I looked at Bryce who was still wearing the same goofy grin, then back at Sydney.

"Bryce is the father."

"That's—great. Really great. Wow. You must be so happy."

"We're getting there."

"Do you have any plans to, uh…"

"Get married? Jesus, Lindsay! I'm pregnant, not legally insane!"

Bryce looked hurt by this comment, and I watched as Sydney's expression softened.

"Well, as far as daddies go, I could have done worse than a kindergarten teacher."

She reached out to take Bryce's hand, and for the first time since I've known either of them, I saw something in both their eyes that looked less like lust than love.

"We're going to take our time. First, exclusive dating and getting to know each other better."

"You must be so excited."

"We are."

"Drew! Sydney and Bryce are having a baby!" I called up the stairs.

"Sweet-as! I'll go fetch us a bottle of champagne." Drew came back downstairs wearing an argyle sweater, and headed to the coat rack to get his jacket.

"Drew! What's gotten into you? It's like you suddenly have ants in your pants."

"You're not worried your ex-fiancée is pregnant as well, are you laddie?" asked Sydney.

"I thought you'd jump at the chance to be a daddy again."

"Well—it's not that I—Shivers! Have I left the upstairs light on?"

"Drew! Sit down. Sydney—stop picking on Drew. He's still my landlord."

"And your friend!"

"Are we going to sit and chat all night then?" asked Bryce.

"Deal!"

I turned to Drew who had a panic-stricken expression on his face.

"I'm not pregnant."

"Thank God," he sighed, dramatically.

I shook my head, then looked at Sydney, and we both burst out laughing.

Onward and Upward

Dear Ben,

For the past couple of weeks, I've been thinking about our email exchange and also about our relationship. I've actually considered your proposal, including the hare-brained idea to send me an engagement ring by FedEx.

You know how much I've wanted to get married—well how could you not, since I was always leaving out bridal magazines on my coffee table while we were together, and dropping less than subtle hints about the "epidemic" of engagements happening every summer. I'm not sure whether you ever noticed all of my bridal dress sketches in the underwear drawer, but those were actually not meant for you to see (as opposed to the engagement ring sketches that I kept in my desk drawer, hoping you might "accidentally" find them).

The truth is, I spent the last two years of our relationship wondering whether "this could be the night" whenever you took me for a romantic walk, or out for dinner. I was really hurt when you broke up with me, and even more hurt when I found out that you had fallen in love and asked someone else to marry you. All I could think was, *Why wasn't it me?*

You can imagine how torn I felt when you emailed with your sudden change of heart after discovering that Marie lied to you. Honestly Ben, I am really sorry that things turned out this way. It sounds like you were both genuinely happy together, at least for a little while.

When I look back on all of our memories together, they still bring a smile to my face. I remember our first date, when you took me for a walk in the park that warm June night, and surprised me by jumping into a water fountain and completely drenching your jeans. I also remember our first kiss at the beach, and the first time we argued (over which TV show took precedence: the season finale of my favorite sitcom or your hockey playoffs). Throughout our four years together, I always considered you to be my very best friend. I thought I must be the luckiest girl in the world to have a handsome pilot, who also understands the need for the occasional container of Haagen Daaz, as my boyfriend.

Despite what I wrote in my emails, I do value your opinion and after I had time to calm down, I thought about your comments about Drew. You're right when you say that our engagement happened quickly (you're also a shameless hypocrite!) They say that guys are the ones who confuse lust with love, but I think I've been guilty of that lately. You'll be happy to know that we won't be getting married after all.

When I woke up this morning, after spending over two weeks thinking about my future and whether it's possible for me to have a fresh beginning, I knew that today would be different somehow. It started off normally enough—I made breakfast for Miles and we watched a Walt Disney DVD together while Drew fussed over himself in the bathroom. Then, as I was trying to pry Miles away from the TV while he admonished me to "be nice," the phone rang. I was expecting it to be Janine, Drew's ex-wife, who usually calls to say something completely inappropriate (it's a long story). Actually, if I didn't know better, I'd say she's become friendly since Drew and I broke up, dropping hints about coming to Canada to visit sometime so that Miles can see his "favourite auntie." She even asked if she could have my chocolate chip cookie recipe so she can bake for Miles after I leave. She must be feeling guilty about all of her threats to chop my hair off (another long story).

Anyway, it wasn't Janine on the phone. It was a woman called Philippa who introduced herself as Bryce's cousin, and told me she had received an article I wrote on "Looking for Mr. Right." It turns out that Bryce had mailed it to her without saying anything to me, and despite the strawberry jam stains (never mind), she loved it! Apparently, Philippa is starting up a new magazine for women, and she asked whether I'd be interested in joining it. She says she's looking for new writers and she'd like to offer me my own column! Can you believe it? I have the chance to write for a magazine! She's going to be in town at the end of the month, so I'll be meeting her to talk about everything then. God knows what my parents will say (and what I'll do with my teaching certificate), but you know me—I always manage to find a way.

After I got the big news, I thought—you know, this is the happiest and most excited I've ever been in my life, including when Drew proposed to me. And that's when it hit me: I don't want to get married anymore. At least, not right now. For the first time in my life, I'm really excited about something and it has nothing to do with men! It's like I'm finally doing what feels right, and what actually makes me happy.

Ben, I don't want you to feel badly about my decision. You know as well as I do that you're stinging from what happened with Marie, and rushing into a sudden commitment with me is not the right answer for either of us. There have been enough hasty engagements this year, all things considered.

I need time to get my life on track, and figure out who I am, when I'm not romantically attached to someone or drowning my sorrows in Haagen Daaz. If that woman turns out to be someone who would even remotely consider taking back an apologetic ex who dumped her for a Barbie doll, you might stand a chance with me.

But not now...I've got dreams to reach.

Love,

Lindsay

Chapter Fourteen

Epilogue
Wives: They're Not Like Us

Wives: They're Not Like Us

By Lindsay Breyer B.A., LL.B.
Creative Writing Instructor, Abbotsford College
In Her Debut Feature Column for Women's Life Magazine

Has anyone besides me ever wondered why married women seem to get all the perks in our society? Not only do magazines like *Us Weekly* glorify the actresses with the multi-million dollar "private" weddings of the century, but they also create the impression that Hollywood singles are secretly living lives of personal hell. Only when a Hollywood starlet is swept off her feet by her leading man, (who may or may not already be married), and then the subject of a much-publicized affair ending in wedding bells, is she considered to be at the very top of Hollywood's "A-list". Why is that?

Now granted, most of us aren't Hollywood stars whose success is measured in terms of movie offers, Oscar goody bags, or the results of public surveys following bizarre appearances on Oprah. But personally, I've felt the sting of denied perks and privileges while living the life of a mere mortal.

My ex-boyfriend, let's call him…"Glen"…is an airline pilot with access to many perks such as free travel around the globe. But, despite the fact that I practically lived with this man for four years, which is longer than most marriages nowadays, I was denied perks such as the following:

- Free travel around the globe
- Health and drug insurance
- Life insurance
- An invitation to the Annual Pilots & Wives Dinner
- Dental Insurance

Why was I not allowed these things, while his colleagues' Better Halves took full advantage of vacationing in the Caribbean six times a year? Because we were not legally married. That's right—those pilots' wives could flit from country to country getting their teeth cleaned on layovers, while I was stuck in the same boring city dodging my dentist's phone calls because I couldn't afford to get my teeth cleaned on my student budget. How fair is that, I ask you?

I performed the duties of a wife: Dealing with the proverbial underwear on the floor, scrubbing more than my fair share of pots and pans (not to mention toilet bowls), and attending family get-togethers that would drive most daughters-in-law to the brink of insanity. I also felt like a wife. I was the most significant other in my boyfriend's world: The one he turned to after a bad day at work; the one who made him chocolate cheesecake for his birthday, and the one who could tell you the exact date his favorite hockey team won the Stanley Cup playoffs.

Unfortunately, despite the passion and strength of our relationship, the most significant thing in my life, to others, it was relatively insignificant.

A sad case in point: On one sweltering hot day in July, Glen and I went to visit his sister Pam after spending the afternoon hiking.

"Come in! Come in!" she greeted us, while the aroma of meatloaf wafted through the doorway. Pam had been busy cooking dinner in the kitchen, while her fourteen year old son played video games in the living room with a friend from school.

"Can I get you something to drink?"

A short time later, while the three of us sat at the kitchen table drinking tall glasses of lemonade with sprigs of mint, Pam suddenly remembered her manners, and asked whether we had met her son's friend, "Ryan".

"Boys!" she called, in her nasally voice.

"Ryan! I want you to come meet Glen and his 'friend.'"

She turned to me with an absentminded expression.

"What's your name again? I was going to call you 'Allison.'"

I blinked several times, unwilling to believe she couldn't remember my name after I'd been dating her brother for the past two years. Clearly, none of my chocolate glazed triple-layer cheesecakes had made the impression I was hoping for. Mental note to self: don't bother making desserts for Glen's family get-togethers anymore.

It's Lindsay, not Allison, I mumbled. *Allison was his girlfriend in high school.*

Afterwards, Glen and I had a heated argument in his parked car, while passers-by sent us curious glances, then sagely hurried away from the lovers' quarrel.

"How can she not know my name? What is wrong with your family? No one ever asks about me, no one makes conversation with me at your stupid family get-togethers..."

"Lindsay, it isn't a conspiracy!" Glen snapped, two bright red spots appearing on his cheeks.

"They're just not—Look. We're not married. They still think of me as single. It's nothing personal against you."

Aha! There it was, rearing its ugly head, yet again: The Married Woman bias. Until Glen proposed with a ring, and walked me down the aisle, his family members would continue to forget my name, and his parents would insist that we sleep in separate bedrooms at their cottage. The fact that I had absolutely zero power over when, or if, Glen ever asked me to marry him (years later after I'd moved to New Zealand, in case you're wondering), was irrelevant.

I've noticed that marriage confers a privileged status on women, as though finagling a diamond ring from Birks and a (supposedly) lifetime commitment of fidelity from a man, is the ultimate validation of our worthiness. Aren't we already worthy? Don't our degrees, our work achievements, our hobbies, and carefully chosen circle of friends, count for anything? *Of course not*, says my Auntie D, who insists the only degree worth having is an "M.R.S." Auntie D, at the ripe old age of 86, God bless her, is convinced that only marriage will make a woman's life complete. I remember receiving the somewhat shocking news that I had actually passed my Bar exams, and calling her in the wee hours of the morning at her home in Yorkshire, England.

"Auntie D! Auntie D!" I yelled into the receiver.

"I've got exciting news for you! Guess what?"

"You're engaged!" she exclaimed.

"What? No—I got called to the Bar. I'm officially a lawyer!"

"Still a spinster," she sighed, with resignation. "Never mind, love. Never mind."

As much as I love my Auntie D, it's these sorts of reactions that make me wonder why, despite all the progress we've made as women, our ultimate source of validation in many people's eyes, only comes from a man.

If Hollywood actresses, who seem to have everything, still need marriage to enjoy the highest status in society, what hope is there for the rest of us? Sure, we might not have to dodge public rumors of homosexuality, but we still have to deal with the Auntie D's of our lives, who privately fret we'll spend our remaining days living in someone's attic, dependent on the crumbs of strangers' kindness. We still have to answer the dreaded "Why aren't you married yet?" question, and mentally deflect the unspoken assumption that apparently, someone's "amiss" because she hasn't yet obtained her "M.R.S."

The truth is, some things in life are overrated, and I have a sneaking suspicion that marriage might be one of them. How else do you explain the fact that so many marriages don't even last? It's not that I have anything against marriage, or even that I believe we shouldn't aspire to be married. But I don't think marriage should confer a privileged status denied to the rest of us, and it also shouldn't make or break our personal happiness.

(For the record, this column is written by a devastatingly attractive and single woman who actually turned down two marriage proposals last year. So you see, it is possible to choose "the single life," as opposed to feeling trapped by it.)

Well, I wanted to end this piece by saying something witty and profound, but I can't seem to think of anything to say except this: whether or not you're sharing the same bedroom with your Significant Other at his parents' cottage, how you see yourself is more important than how anyone else sees you. And if your Significant Other leaves his underwear on the bedroom floor like my ex-fiancé Drew, just remember—it's always his responsibility to pick them up!

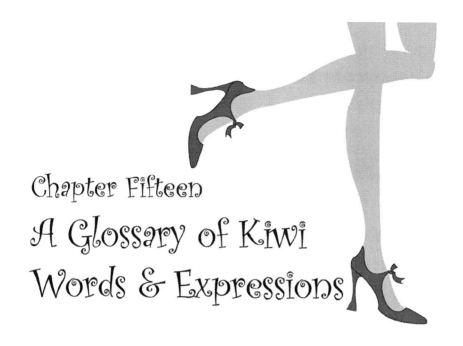

Chapter Fifteen
A Glossary of Kiwi Words & Expressions

A GLOSSARY OF KIWI WORDS & EXPRESSIONS

a into g: to get going (arse into gear)
Helena used to say, "Put your A into G!" every morning when I was running late for school or practicum.

arse: rear end, butt, ass
As in, Jennifer Lopez is generally considered to have a very nice arse, or "President Bush is a right arse!" as George used to say.

B

banger: sausage
Bryce was always buying expensive bangers at the grocery store instead of fruit and vegetables.

biscuit: cookie

bloody-hell: all-purpose expletive
Another favorite expression of George.
As in, "Do you still reckon you're in Australia? Bloody-hell, you Americans are stupid!"

boot: car trunk
Drew and I used to keep Miles' toys in the boot of the car while traveling with him.

bugger all: not much, very little

bun-fight: social gathering with food
As in, one of our classmates Morris decided to "come out of the closet" at Sydney's bun-fight, whereupon he had a panic attack and ran away into the night, never to be seen nor heard from again.

C

capsicum: bell pepper

car park: parking lot

chat-up: to flirt, to try pick-up lines on someone you "fancy." As in, Lydia wanted to wring her husband's neck for chatting me up at Sydney's bun-fight.

cheeky: sassy, impish, insolent or impudent
As in, it was cheeky of Bryce to ask me for favors when he was being such an arse to me.

cheers: good-bye; thank-you
About a month after sending my letter of complaint to Principal Henry Whittaker, I received the following note in the mail:

Dear Lindsay,
Thank you for your rather unusual letter.
I understand that you've had some difficulty in making a smooth transition to
student life in New Zealand. Perhaps an attitude adjustment might be in order.
I wish you a pleasant and safe stay in Wellington.
Cheers,
Henry

chemist: pharmacy
As in, Drew and I bought no-frill condoms from the chemist.

chips: French fries
Drew was excited to find a great fish and chip shop where he and Miles
and I could all eat for under $5.

choice: very good

crisps: potato chips

D

dag: An amusing person or situation (colloq).
dairy: convenience store
The place where I bought most of my Magnum ice-cream bars and orange
vodka coolers.
You can also buy a packet of "crisps" (potato chips) and a bottle of "fizzy"
(soda pop) from the dairy.

dodgy: suspicious; a person with questionable motives
As in, Bryce seemed like a bit of a dodgy character in the beginning
because he claimed he had been traveling for the past seventeen years
since graduating from high school. I think he stole my Tommy Hilfiger
sunglasses as well.

dole: unemployment benefit; state funded income support

duvet: quilt

F

fancy: to find attractive, to have a romantic interest in someone
As in, Drew accused me of fancying my form teacher, Shane who ended up leaving Frieda's Finishing School to pursue his true passion as judge on New Zealand's Next Top Model.

flash: sensational
The words seems to connote "nice" or "expensive" and "flashy". The way Paris Hilton tends to dress.

flat: apartment

football: rugby
As in, the All Blacks are New Zealand's football team, and because of them, I missed the season finale of *Friends*.

fortnight: fourteen days, two weeks
The length of time it took for me to realize that only two people can have a shower at Drew's house before the hot water runs out.

full on: intense
As in, Miles is full-on right now. (Miles is a handful right now)
Or, classes are full on.

G

good on ya, mate!: congratulations
What Drew should have said when good friends of ours announced their pregnancy. Instead, he nearly had a panic attack à la Morris from Sydney's bun-fight.

gumboots: large rubber overshoes ranging from calf to knee height. These are usually black, although little children may wear colorful ones.

H

heaps: general expression to mean a lot, as in "miss you heaps," or try hard; "give it heaps"
As in, deciding to get involved with Drew landed me in heaps of trouble with his ex-wife.

hottie: hot water bottle
As in, there is no central heating in New Zealand so you have to sleep with a hottie at night to stay warm (ha ha).

K

Kiwi: New Zealander
kiwi: an endangered flightless bird native to New Zealand
kiwifruit: kiwi (formerly known as Chinese gooseberry)
kia ora: Maori for hello
knackered: Exhausted (from Knacker, an archaic profession whose practitioners destroyed old horses)
How I used to feel after a night of sexual gymnastics with Drew.
knickers: underwear
kornies: Kellogs cornflakes
kumara: sweet potato/yam

L
lemonade: clear soda (7Up)
lift: elevator
lolly: candy
lolly scramble:: a festive search for candies (lollies)
loo: bathroom
lorry: truck
lounge: living room
M
main: primary dish of a meal
Maori: indigenous people of New Zealand
mate: buddy, pal
a mission: A difficult undertaking
mobile: cell phone
money for jam: easy money
motorway: freeway
N
nappy: diaper
netball: game somewhat similar to basketball
no worries: not a problem

P

paddled: to lose or to suffer ill fate.

How I felt when I first arrived in New Zealand.

pakeha: non-Maori person

party pooper: being negative

petrol: gasoline

piece-of-piss: easy

pike out: to give up when the going gets tough

(What I didn't do while I was living through the eighth circle of hell, known as George's International Languages class.)

pikelet: small pancake often served with jam and whipped cream

piker: one who gives up easily (see pike-out)

pissed: drunk, inebriated

pissed-off: angry

piss-up: social gathering with alcohol

PMT (Pre Menstrual Tension): PMS

pom: English person, slang

power cut: outage

postal code: zip code

pram: baby carriage, stroller

pub: bar

rack off: go away (angry)

R

randy: horny, feeling sexual impulses

A good description for Drew's mood, most hours of the day.

ratbag: scally-wag, somewhat annoying person

redundant: to be laid off, "workers were made redundant today"

right as rain: perfect

ring: phone/call

rockmelon: cantaloupe

rooted: to feel tired

rough as guts: unpolished (referring to a person)

round the bend: going crazy/busy

As in, Janine drove me round the bend with her maddening telephone calls and messages.

rubber: eraser

rubbish: trash/garbage

<u>S</u>

shandy: drink made with lemonade and beer

Sheila: woman (outdated expression)

She'll be right: things will be fine

snarky: mixture of sarcastic and nasty

sook: a moody person. "Don't worry about him, he's just a big sook".

spot on: exactly right

stirrer: trouble-maker, agitator

stroppy: bad tempered

As in, George was a stroppy old arse who hates Americans.

supper: late evening coffee/desserts

suss: to figure out

As in, I should have spent more time sussing out the details of my international teaching program before deciding to study in Wellington.

<u>T</u>

ta: Thanks

take away: take out

take the piss: to ridicule

tea: dinner—generic name for evening meal

tea towel: dish rag

tracksuit: sweats

togs: swimsuit

tomato sauce: catsup

torch: flashlight

trolley: shopping cart

<u>W</u>

wally: incompetent person, loser

wanker: (derogatory, impolite) jerk, loser

Sadly, the best way to describe most of the guys I've dated.

wardrobe: clothes closet

whinge: complain

The best thing about doing what makes you truly happy, is that if you're single you'll find you don't whinge nearly as much about it.

Wicked: cool

Made in the USA